OUTLAW

BY DONALD WILLERTON

Ghosts of the San Juan

The Lost Children

The Secret of La Rosa

The Hidden River

The Lake of Fire

OUTLAW

A MOGI FRANKLIN MYSTERY

BOOK 6

DONALD WILLERTON

WISE WOLF
BOOKS

Outlaw
Paperback Edition
Copyright © 2025 (As Revised) Donald Willerton

Wise Wolf Books
An imprint of Wolfpack Publishing
1707 E. Diana Street Tampa, FL 33610

wisewolfbooks.com

Paperback ISBN 978-1-965596-99-9
eBook ISBN 978-1-965596-98-2

For My Mother

OUTLAW

CHAPTER 1

SOUTHEASTERN WYOMING, JUNE 2, 1899

Drenched by heavy sheets of blowing, near-freezing rain, the Union Pacific Overland Flyer Number One pulled next to the water tower in Rock River, Wyoming, at about 2 a.m. Guided by a lantern, the shivering, barrel-chested fireman caught the let-down rope whipping in the wind, stepped to the back of the coal tender, and pulled hard on the spout to lower it into the opening of the water tank.

Inside the cab, the train's engineer blew small, even puffs of smoke from his pipe as he patiently watched.

When the water burped out of the opening, the fireman played out the rope as the spout's counterweight pulled it back upright, flopped the lid over the tank's hole, and tightened it down. Muttering curses about the rain, the wind, the cold, and the darkness, he returned to shoveling coal into the firebox.

The engineer pulled hard on the whistle and leaned into his control lever. With agonizing slowness, the engine, pulling two express cars, three passenger coaches, and a caboose, struggled forward with the harsh sound of steam pounding against pistons. Coming up to speed, the engine was back to slicing through the curtains of rain, hard on its way to Wilcox station, a tiny piece of civilization in the middle of the Wyoming wilderness.

A few minutes later, the engineer saw three swinging lanterns ahead in the darkness. On a night like this, it would not have been unusual for a stream to have risen and taken out a bridge or part of the track, so the engineer immediately slacked off the steam and applied the brakes, the heavy iron wheels jerking and sputtering as the train slowed.

But instead of delivering a warning about a washed-out track, three masked men quickly jumped onto the locomotive's steps, forcing their way up with pistols in their hands. Holding the barrel of his gun against the engineer's ear, one of the men directed him to pull the train ahead of a short trestle in front of them, which he did. Then he watched as the trestle was blown to smithereens.

One of the men ran back beyond the last express car, uncoupled the following car, and mounted the back platform, signaling that his job was done. The train was driven further a couple more miles, where three more men on horseback rode in beside the tracks, pulling saddled horses behind them.

The first express car was ransacked but revealed nothing of value. The guard inside the second express car, a loyal railroad employee named Charles Woodcock, refused to open the locked express car door. A stick of dynamite later, the door and a dazed Woodcock lay in a pile of splinters. Without Woodcock to provide the combination to the huge safe inside, one of the outlaws grew impatient and placed three sticks of dynamite on the handle of the safe.

The blast not only blew the door off the safe but also blew most of the top and sides of the express car a hundred feet into the countryside. As the smoke cleared, hundreds of currency bills mixed with the rain as they fluttered back to earth. The outlaws gathered what remained, packed it into their saddlebags, and galloped into the darkness.

Three of the outlaws headed toward Casper, and three others toward Lander. Over the next three days, sometimes together, sometimes splitting apart and then rejoining, each group of outlaws raced along various trails through the Wyoming countryside, riding hundreds of miles in a weaving pattern. As planned beforehand, they found fresh mounts and food at friendly ranches and towns.

Within a day or two, the best trackers and lawmen in the country were chasing anyone and everyone connected to the Wilcox holdup. The Union Pacific refused to officially reveal how much had been stolen. A later report, however, stated, "The six outlaws had gathered unsigned bank notes, considerable cash, nineteen scarf pins, twenty-nine gold-plated cuff button pairs, and four new Elgin watches." Eventually, Union Pacific admitted that more than $50,000 had been taken, including a significant amount in gold coins. The haul was huge—sufficient to make the six outlaws very happy.

After three harrowing days and nights on the run and giving the slip to every lawman after them, the bandits came together at Anderson's hog ranch, close to the crossing of the Little Muddy River between Fort Washakie and Thermopolis, where they divided the loot.

Harvey Logan, the man who held the pistol to the engineer's ear, had been in charge of the robbery and was voted to get first pick. He had no use for scarf pins or cuff buttons, but selected one of the fancy pocket watches, the face circled with diamonds and outfitted with the newest innovation in watch design: a stem-winding mechanism.

It was a watch far more beautiful than any of the men had seen. Of course, he also took a pile of money.

Another man, called Butch Cassidy, the leader of the Wild Bunch gang and the planner of the train robbery, took a different pile of money and then selected a diamond-studded watch just like Harvey's. The rest of the men quickly took care of the remaining money and jewelry.

Someone sent for a wagon full of fun-loving women from a nearby town, and they all soon devoted themselves to having a good time. After a long night of drinking, dancing, playing cards, and roasting an elk, most of the gang rode south for New Mexico while others split in different directions.

Harvey Logan rode directly to Brown's Hole, a hideout in a wide valley on the border of Utah and Colorado, straddling the Green River. Two days later, well-rested and trailing a string of fresh horses, he went south into the vast rock mazes of southern Utah. Hidden in the middle of twisted canyons, massive mesas, and confusing valleys was Robber's Roost, the last hideout along the Outlaw Trail.

It was known to the lawmen of that area, but the country was so rough, so bewildering, so effective at hiding men and horses, and especially so easy to defend against anyone not welcome, that the law knew to avoid it.

Finally reaching the ranch in a maze of canyons and mesas, Harvey met up with Butch and Harry Longabaugh, known as the Sundance Kid. The next day, Butch and Sundance left the Roost, descending westward from the mesa tops into the vast array of canyons making up the drainage basin of the Colorado River. Following the different valleys, they eventually headed up a secret trail out of the bare rock country to a ranch in eastern Utah.

Two days after they had left, Harvey set out on the same trail as Butch and Sundance. He had not been through the country before and closely followed Butch's instructions. He walked his horses down the steep and difficult trail into the valley of the Dirty Devil River and then, at a place with a solid bottom, crossed and continued south for several miles until he reached Cass Hite's ferry on the west side of the Colorado River.

Crossing to the east side of the river, Harvey searched for White Canyon. An unremarkable canyon from the river's edge, White Canyon was the only canyon in the hundreds of square miles of twisting rock that had a trail where a man and horse could ride out of the canyonlands into the relatively flat country of eastern Utah. From a high point back at the Roost, Butch had pointed in the distance at the different canyon openings along the route that Harvey should go. At the time, the way seemed obvious. But when Harvey found himself on the riverbank, he was soon bewildered, now utterly dependent on the sign that Butch had placed at the White Canyon entrance.

Take a sacred oath.

That was the secret phrase Butch had given him. It matched a drawing that Butch had carved into the sandstone wall at the entrance of White Canyon, the only mark that distinguished it from the dozens of other canyons. Those who knew how to match the phrase to the drawing could identify the correct canyon opening, all others would ride right by.

"When you get across the Colorado at Hite's ferry, ride south on the east bank until you see the sign to take a sacred oath."

Harvey Logan muttered a long curse about Butch Cassidy and his secret phrases as he searched the sandstone walls.

CHAPTER 2

LAKE POWELL, PRESENT DAY

Except for putting on his weight belt, Mogi Franklin was ready. The other students were still milling around the deck, sorting out tanks, buckles, straps, respirators, depth gauges, chalkboards, knives, masks, and other equipment. Proud of being so quick to get his gear together, Mogi leaned against the houseboat's railing and looked across the lake as heat waves radiated off the rock cliffs surrounding Farley Canyon Bay.

Let's go, people! he was thinking. *We've been at this for three days—you should be faster by now!*

Called *slickrock country*, southern Utah was an immense land of twisted canyons and tilted mesas. It was as if thick, cream-colored cake frosting had been smeared in thousand-foot layers over hundreds of square miles of earth and then sculpted with a heavenly butter knife to make swirls, dips, and slices. But it was solid rock instead of cake frosting, and the swirls, dips, and slices made up a vast empire of mountains, winding valleys, gullies, canyons, and tall, isolated buttes. Void of vegetation except in the dirt-filled bottoms of the deepest canyons, the country was famous for its smooth, bald surfaces of sandstone.

To the south, 135 miles from where Mogi stood, Glen Canyon Dam spanned a steep-walled canyon to block the mighty Colorado River. Built in 1961, it took almost five years to reach its full capacity as the tall, thick, concrete dam backed the river water into that vast empire of stone to form Lake Powell, one of the largest man-made lakes in the world.

With more shoreline by some accounts than the state of California and more than ninety individual canyons flooded with water, Lake Powell was an oasis for boating, fishing, water skiing, hiking, and camping that drew people from all over the world. The deep, calm, expansive waters were a haven for thousands of people who vacationed in rented houseboats—mini-houses, sitting on top of monstrous aluminum pontoons, with bedrooms, living rooms, bathrooms, kitchens, and second floors of open-air decks. One or two massive outboard motors powered the crafts through the water.

The warm water, nearly clear conditions, and abundance of places to explore had also made Lake Powell one of the best places in the Southwest for scuba diving.

"Get your weight belts and we'll go through our checklist," the instructor called out.

Mogi muscled his way into the small crowd with a hunched-over swagger, his upper body leaning forward to balance the heavy tank strapped to his back.

The weight belts were hung on a rack next to the stairs, each belt a wide nylon strap with lead weights attached. On the first day of class, every student was assigned a particular belt, to which weights were then added or taken off, depending on the person's weight. Buckled around each diver's waist, the weight of the lead made up for the natural buoyancy of the diver in the water. Without it, a diver would have a difficult time staying beneath the surface of the water, in spite of the weight of the tank and other equipment.

Mogi sorted through the labels for his own weight belt, found a few without labels, tried to be polite to the other hands picking through the belts, didn't see his own label, and finally grabbed one that looked like what he'd worn the day before.

"Tank centered, straps tight, buckles clipped in, respirator in front and tested, depth gauge, tank gauge, watches in place, weight belt secure, fins, safety knife strapped and secure, dive mask…" The instructor went down the equipment checklist, looking across the group for nodding heads.

Mogi had jumped at the chance to learn to scuba dive.

A month before, an adventure outfitter in Flagstaff advertised a four-day scuba class at Lake Powell.

Since the lake was only about ninety miles from his home in Bluff, a small town in the southeast part of Utah close to the famous Four Corners area, it was an easy decision for him to sign up. It took more effort to convince his sister, Jennifer, to do it, but when their parents worked out a deal for free housing during the days of the class, plus the weekends before and after, she finally agreed.

The McDowells were longtime family friends who owned a houseboat and a smaller speedboat at Lake Powell, keeping them docked at Hite Marina when not in use. In exchange for staying on the houseboat, Mogi and Jennifer would do some cleaning and minor repairs, working through a list of improvements that the McDowells had planned but never done.

Back in his position, leaning against the railing, waiting as the instructors helped others with their equipment, Mogi grew increasingly impatient with the slow, methodical procedures of the instructors.

Let's go, people! he continued to think. *Quit talking, and let's get going!*

The class started on Sunday, a week before the Fourth of July weekend. The eight students gathered each morning at Hite Marina, located at the very north end of Lake Powell, and were then shuttled by speedboats to a large houseboat anchored in Farley Canyon, four miles south.

The houseboat served as the center of operations. The largest model available for rent at the lake, the bedrooms housed the instructors, the equipment, and the food needed for the class. The kitchen and living room provided space for lunches and snacks. The large deck over the living area provided the space to store, sort, clean, repair, and issue the diving equipment and also served as the classroom. The area at the back of the houseboat served as the staging area to get divers in and out of the water.

At the end of each daily session, in the late afternoon, the students were motored back to the marina. While Jennifer and Mogi stayed on the McDowells' houseboat, the others went back to their tents or RVs at the nearby campground.

After six training dives, a few lectures, a written exam, and a final qualifying dive passed successfully, each participant would qualify for scuba certification.

"Everybody, listen up," the instructor said, "and let's go through the safety briefing, like we do every time we enter the water. You must always be conscious of safety. Number one, never, ever get in a hurry. Two, know what equipment you have and be sure that everything is working. Three, check your tank gauge to know that you have a full tank. Four…"

Mogi knew the briefing by heart. He could recite it if asked. Giving the instructor minimal attention, he looked over the railing and watched the water, hoping to see fish and wondering how expensive it would be to buy a spear gun. Going after fish with a spear gun would be pretty cool.

"Six, if something goes wrong, you each have a slim-style emergency inflation vest, so pull the red cord and hold on, you'll get to the surface pretty quick. Seven…"

The water was remarkably clear, the details of the lake bottom plainly visible even though it was ten feet beneath the boat. A big bass swam by. Mogi imagined zinging it with a spear and plopping it into a frying pan.

"We've practiced how to stay oriented below the surface," the instructor continued. "Today, we're going deeper than we have, down to fifty feet. Everybody needs to be on their toes. We picked this bay because there's a wide shelf around the shoreline, but we're going beyond it to get our fifty feet of depth. That will be closer to the middle of the bay, where the water is around two hundred feet deep. You won't see a bottom anymore, and it'll be pretty dark, so stay with your partner and pay attention."

After a few more instructions, one by one, each diver shuffled to the back of the boat and stepped down onto a platform tied alongside. They awkwardly put on their fins, turned around and squatted, took a firm hold of their masks and respirators, and fell backward into the water, disappearing beneath the surface.

Mogi followed the others. After sliding on his fins and tightening up the straps, he stood up, feeling like a fully equipped warrior. Then he squatted, tipped backward, and was soon in the water, angling forward to come up beside Jennifer. He already felt more coordinated and confident than the day before.

In fact, he felt powerful.

He swallowed to equalize the pressure in his ears. The instructor swam along the shore, with the students lining out behind him. The frog-awkwardness that everyone had displayed on the boat was replaced with slowly and smoothly swaying fins, with columns of bubbles swirling up from the respirators.

Mogi kept Jennifer on his left. He admired how graceful she was. To her, swimming was just another form of dancing, and she was really good at dancing.

Mogi was fourteen and tall for his age, but his muscles had not yet caught up with his bones, so he was gangly and spindly and a little bit awkward, which is to say, normal for his position in life. But he was smarter than most, which gave him some comfort. He took after his mom's side of the family with his looks and his shyness, but seemed to be a sum of both families on the brain side—he was smart, quick-minded, mentally disciplined, and orderly, and had a natural talent for solving puzzles.

Jennifer, at seventeen, was his opposite. She definitely took after their father. Shorter than her brother by a half-foot, with thick, brown hair cut short, she was strong, athletic, and graceful, had a keen sense of human nature, and loved being around people. While Mogi was the obsessive, analytical, adventurous problem-solver, Jennifer was the cautious, emotionally centered people person. He pushed her to do more than she thought she ought to, she pulled him back into what was reasonable.

Oh, yeah, and he didn't have a driver's license yet, so that's why he had to make sure she took the scuba class.

The filtered sunlight from above jumped and

shook and wiggled across the backs of the swimmers ahead of him. Below, the shimmering light died in the soft mud, where a scattering of rocks and submerged logs gave a jumbled texture to the silt-covered sandstone shelf.

Everything lost its color, appearing dim and dull under a layer of mud.

Mogi looked side to side and listened to the gurgle of his respirator.

The previous days' training drills had gradually increased the depth, the time, and the distances the students swam. Combining increasingly difficult dives with lectures—about equipment, water, air, buoyancy, how pressure works, and the dangers of diving—most of the students were now comfortable with their equipment and the out-of-this-world experience of moving under water.

After gagging a few times and panicking once or twice the first day, Mogi had settled into a comfortable groove.

Piece of cake.

The instructors gave hand signals and turned toward the center of the bay. Everyone moved out from over the sloped shelf, watched the edge of the rocks pass below them, and swam into the emptiness.

Mogi immediately sensed the decreased light. Everything on the sides of the submerged canyon walls—the rim, the rock layers, the mud—dropped out of sight below him, fading into the darkness. It surprised and frightened him. He instinctively swam upward, as if to escape a force pulling him downward.

The group descended in a slow spiral. The instructors stopped the group at thirty, then forty, and then fifty feet, each time motioning for everyone to check their gauges and watches.

At fifty feet, the craggy features of the rock layers of the wall beside Mogi turned soft and appeared as if covered by fog, the lack of light dimming the whole scene.

Jennifer was beside him, now upright, slowly moving her fins to keep herself at a constant depth. She checked her pressure gauge and watch, looked at him with a sense of awe, and then slowly twirled around.

She nudged him as the instructors motioned for each pair of partners to swim in a circle, and he fell in beside her as they found the rhythm of their kicks. He struggled to keep at her level, using his arms to swim upward as she glided along. His breath was coming in short heaves, and he focused to keep his respirator at a constant gurgle. It was surprisingly more work than what he had found the day before.

There was a muted clanging sound. The instructor used the handle of her dive knife to bang against her tank, the signal for everyone to come together. It was time to ascend back to ten feet, check everyone out, and then descend again.

Mogi followed Jennifer as she headed upward, checking gauges at the various levels. He had been impressed the day before at how well he and his sister were attuned to each other, how smoothly they worked together. But he was now pumping hard to keep up with her. At the ten-foot depth, expecting to relax and hang beside her, he kept drifting downward instead, having to sometimes kick his fins to come back to her side. He didn't remember that from the day before.

When everyone gave the thumbs-up sign, the group descended again. Each pair of partners would spiral directly to fifty feet, spend another five minutes in a circular pattern, ascend to the surface, and then get back on the houseboat.

One last lecture about handling diving emergencies was scheduled after lunch, and another dive afterward, which left only the qualification dive the next morning. Mogi was tired. He looked forward to being back on the boat and taking off all his gear, and it would be lunchtime, too, which was always a high point of the day.

He and Jennifer spiraled downward as the hazy canyon sides once again moved past them. Though he didn't intend to, he had soon left Jennifer in the water above him.

At forty feet, he knew something was wrong.

When he had to give several hard kicks to level out at fifty feet, he felt sweat dripping from his eyebrows inside his mask. Bile rose in his throat as he kicked his legs back and forth. His depth gauge reading dropped to fifty-five and then to sixty feet. He pumped his legs hard, straining at pushing the fins through the water, powering as much as he could. But in spite of the extra effort, Mogi continued to slip down, deeper into the darkness below.

Jennifer swam furiously toward him, pulling at his hands but unable to stop his descent. She grabbed her dive knife and banged it hard against her tank.

Mogi panicked. He doubled his efforts, his fins swinging furiously, his arms frantically stroking for the surface.

His legs felt like lead, and his thighs burned with every movement. He struggled to remain upright. It was almost too dark to read the depth gauge, but he saw that it had moved to seventy, and then to seventy-five.

He beat against the water, fighting to follow his bubbles, resisting the thoughts of what he had been told about scuba divers who went too deep: eyes bulging, eardrums exploding…

His energy finally drained and he went limp, the blackness swallowing him.

He felt only a small bump when a body crashed against him, reached around his tank, and pulled on the red cord attached to his harness. There was an immediate jerk, and his exhausted body felt relief as it quit sinking and started rising toward the surface. Suspended in a netherworld of exhaustion, he no longer recognized what was happening or why.

As the instructor held onto his harness from the back, Mogi glanced down through the bubbles streaming across his mask. With his head feeling somehow detached from his body, he idly watched as a strange fish swam toward him from below.

It was a funny-shaped, multicolored fish, unlike any he had ever seen. The fish seemed to pause and then drifted backward. Through the gray of the dark, Mogi noticed a light glowing from the fish. Not all over, just a distorted pattern of light from the top.

Mogi slowly realized that from inside the light on top of the funny fish, a man's face stared back at him.

CHAPTER 3

"**D**on't worry about it. It was a stupid mistake, but you survived. You won't do it again." Mogi had put on the wrong weight belt. It had the same number of lead weights as his correct belt, so it kind of looked the same, but four of the weights were twice as heavy as the normal weights. So, after wearing out his muscles struggling to stay level, he had dropped like a rock.

And he had forgotten about his inflatable rescue vest.

Stupid.

Instructors always wished for some fool to do something really dumb so they could use the incident to illustrate what *not* to do. His story would last for years.

Stupid!

Mogi leaned his elbows on the table and stretched his back. At least the last dive of the day had gone without mishap. Tomorrow, he'd be certified. Then he could do what he wanted without witnesses.

"Are you still interested in the visitor center movie?" he asked.

"I'll do anything to get out of this heat," Jennifer replied. "The next time we swap work for a week on a houseboat, let's make sure the air conditioner works. It's like an oven in here. Let's go. We can get something to eat at Bullfrog. You have the map?"

Mogi traced the route as Jennifer drove out of the Hite Marina parking lot. They'd go north a couple of miles, cross a bridge over the Colorado River at the very top of Lake Powell, and then go west over the Dirty Devil River. Turning south after that, they would drive to the Glen Canyon Recreation Area Visitor Center at the Bullfrog Marina.

Jennifer and Mogi pulled into the parking lot an hour later, but the temperature hadn't noticeably cooled—it was still in the triple digits. As they entered the visitor center, they found cool air but were immediately jammed into a crowd of people. Outside the auditorium door, a man and a woman were partially blocking the entrance, holding signs calling for the destruction of the dam and the draining of Lake Powell. Inside the auditorium, several others held up more signs, shouting, "Take the dam out!"

"Give us the canyon back!" and "Who are we to destroy beauty?"

Mogi watched as two park rangers tried to quiet them down, or move them to the side, or anything to keep them from disrupting the presentation, but it was no use.

The protestors were doing what protestors do—arousing emotions in support of their cause, usually through in-your-face confrontation.

It's not like the movie is offensive, Mogi thought. It's the same movie that's been showing for the past fifty years: the history of the building of the dam, the filling of the lake, and how much Lake Powell and the dam's electric generation plant supported the irrigation and power needs of the western United States.

Even after the movie started, the noise continued. Most of the visitors gave up and walked out, but not without some name-calling and shoving. More national park rangers appeared, but they only helped to make the exodus more orderly.

Mogi picked up one of the leaflets the protestors handed out.

"I can't even imagine," he said to Jennifer as they walked out. "Destroying the dam and draining Lake Powell? You know what the canyons would look like after being underwater for fifty years? What are these people thinking?"

He found some of the answers as he read the leaflet.

The hundreds of miles of beautiful canyons would be restored through nature, it said, although it would take a hundred years or so for natural rainfall to wash away the mud. Los Angeles would be stopped from robbing the Southwest of its resources, as most of the electricity and a large amount of the water currently went to Southern California. Returning the Colorado River to its natural condition would help restore and preserve the ecosystems of the Grand Canyon, as well as allow the rediscovery of submerged archaeological sites.

"Some of it makes sense," Mogi said to Jennifer as they drove back to Hite Marina, "as long as you don't live in Southern California." He still didn't think draining the lake would be worth it because the then-empty canyons, with their decades of deep mud and silt, would be almost impossible to navigate on foot, which would be the only way that people could reach them. Beautiful geologic features might be revealed when the water drained away, but far fewer people would see them than those who enjoyed the lake now.

———

Mogi was up bright and early the next morning, urging his sister to hurry up. It was graduation day, and the instructors had promised a new adventure for the final dive.

Riding the speedboat to the adventure company's houseboat, it was soon apparent what they had meant. The operations houseboat had been driven to the next bay over, a longer, narrower bay formed by White Canyon, so that the qualifying dive and ceremony would be in new waters.

After a written exam, all students were required to independently outfit themselves, check the operation of their equipment, perform all the safety checks, enter the water alone, swim an underwater circuit, and perform a set of maneuvers that had them descending and ascending through various depths.

A little cake and ice cream, the signing of certificates, and it would be done.

White Canyon Bay was more dramatic, both above and below the water, than the bay of Farley Canyon—steeper walls, more curves and coves, more variations in the colors of the sandstone, and more narrow crevices. It was also more remote, so there was less boat traffic to interfere with their diving activities. Only one other houseboat was anchored in the bay, and it was apparently unoccupied. Mogi gave it a good looking over as he ate his cake.

It was, to say the least, strange-looking.

It was much smaller than the one he was on and obviously many years older. The roof and sides were completely covered with tilted solar panels. Having solar panels on a houseboat wasn't surprising—many people used solar power to charge the batteries of their electrical systems—but this many was extreme. The houseboat itself was barely visible under the shroud of panels.

Only a small fishing boat tied next to the outboard motor showed that someone used the houseboat. Mogi assumed that it belonged to fishermen who used a speedboat to prowl the hot fishing spots of the various canyons.

They typically left before sunrise and didn't return until evening.

"We're getting ready to go back to the marina," Jennifer said to Mogi as she joined him at the railing. "Get your stuff."

Mogi retrieved his bag with his towels, sunscreen, water bottles, and snacks and made his way over to the ladder.

He glanced back to the small houseboat.

It was sinking.

He watched more closely.

Was it really sinking?

It *was* sinking! The whole houseboat!

Then it stopped.

He *must* have been mistaken. But he had looked up at just the right time to see the bow lined up with one of the alternating brown and white layers of sandstone directly behind the boat. As he watched, the deck had suddenly moved below the layers by about a foot. The small houseboat now sat substantially lower in the water, its pontoons half-submerged.

Then that was it. No sound, no ripples, no movement, nothing.

It just sat there.

"Why is your mouth open?" Jennifer asked.

"Did you see that? Did you see that houseboat sink deeper into the water?"

Jennifer looked. "Nope," she replied. "Come on, let's go."

The students filed into the speedboat tied alongside the larger craft and were soon on their way.

Mogi couldn't help but stare at the strange houseboat as they passed by. In the midst of the solar panels, barely visible through the front window glass above the steering wheel, a face looked out.

Mogi's mouth again dropped open.

He had seen the face before—in the darkness of the deep water of Farley Bay, in the light on top of a really funny-looking fish.

CHAPTER 4

The latch made a loud click as the door closed. The man slid the deadbolt across and hung the chain in its slot.

He turned around slowly and looked into the room, moving little more than his eyes. He peeked warily around the bathroom door, softly pushing it open with his bag.

It was an ordinary hotel bathroom. A sink, a toilet, a bathtub. A shower curtain pulled back. The man moved a few steps ahead, hesitant, as if expecting someone to jump out of the corners.

It was an ordinary hotel room. Two queen-sized beds, a wood-like veneer cabinet mounted between them, old bedcovers. A telephone, a two-light sconce, ugly pictures. Small desk in the far corner, cheap desk lamp, ratty desk chair. In-wall air conditioning unit, chest of drawers with TV on top. Old drawstring curtains, faded wallpaper, popcorn texture on the ceiling.

Breathe. Relax. Focus. Everything is okay.

It was still a half-minute before the man crossed the room and placed his bag on the first bed. He put his hands up to his face, pressed hard to stop the jitters, and spoke to himself: It's a room. Just a room. A public, anybody-can-come-and-go hotel room. For tonight, it is my room.

I paid for it. I chose to rent it, and I will stay here. I did not have to ask.

No one checked me, no one patted me down, no one told me what to do, no one told me what not to do, no one told me who to be. I was inside. Now I'm outside.

It's all okay.

Breathe. Relax. Focus. Everything is okay.

Letting out a deep breath, the man opened his bag, removed each of the folded shirts, and hung them in the closet. He removed and hung a pair of neatly folded jeans.

His socks and underwear, all carefully packed, would stay in the bag. Putting them in a drawer was unnecessary.

He'd get things as he needed them. He wouldn't be in the room that long.

He moved the bag to the floor, checked the settings on the air conditioner, and stood next to the window. He pulled the curtains back only enough to see the goings-on outside. The Wahweap Hotel and Marina, on the south end of Lake Powell, looked active, but calm and orderly.

A few people moved about the hotel sidewalks, but

most were busy on the long marina docks extending from the lake shoreline below the hotel. They were shuffling bags, coolers, carts, and other things from cars in the parking area into fishing boats and houseboats.

He watched carefully, noticing each person, trying to see if any glanced toward his room, toward his window, or toward him.

He was a small man, thin, with a ghostly pallor, as pale as if he avoided the sun, but he was not frail. His arms and shoulders were sculpted with firm muscles, and he stood with a military posture. His hair, so light-colored it was hard to see, was cut short and severe. He had no facial hair, and his cheekbones stood out from his eyes, which were slightly sunken within their sockets. Even so, his look was one of intensity, his eyes direct and unblinking, almost scary.

He wore a plain white T-shirt—no pocket, clean—and his new jeans still held their stiffness. One of his first purchases had been an iron, which he used on his clothes after every washing to create perfect creases.

He had shunned tattoos. Unlike the other inmates, whose boredom and vanity resulted in their bodies looking like crowded billboards, he refused the idea. He wanted to be unnoticeable, maybe even invisible if he needed to be.

Nothing different, nothing unusual, nothing to remember, nothing that witnesses could swear to. Maybe once he became known, but not now. Until his works had revealed who he was, he wanted to fade into the background.

Surveying the room again, the man returned to the door, pushed his foot against the bottom, unbolted it, slid the chain off, and rotated the handle. After a moment, he moved his foot and slowly opened the door, peeking through the crack as it widened, and then waited again, listening for any movement. Satisfied that no one lurked in the hallway, he stepped out and pulled the door behind him, testing the handle to make sure the door had closed and locked. He walked quickly and silently down the hallway and stairs and returned to the panel van outside.

He removed two more luggage bags.

Returning to the room, the austere little man locked and secured the door, cautiously observed the inside of the room again, and then proceeded to unpack the larger of the two bags. Out came comic books, gently extracted from the bag one at a time and carefully placed into piles on the second bed. Neatly stacked, in sequence by issue number, one stack per hero. The man was proud, it was quite a collection. He had spent years choosing the right heroes, pulling all the stories together, buying the best editions. He knew every issue in his mind and in his heart.

Once the comics lay in neat lines and rows, once he had established his shrine, he closed the empty bag and set it on the floor next to the chest. He scooted the desk in front of the window, rolled the chair in place, pulled the drapes back fully, and then sat, taking in the full view of the lake and marina.

There was considerable hustle and bustle, the

typical increase of vacationers coming for the extended Fourth of July weekend.

A smile came to the man's face. There'll be more fireworks than they expect, he thought. It will be a Fourth of July to remember.

It is my destiny.

It is who I am.

Having calmed himself with deep breathing and meditation, the man stood and stretched, feeling the fatigue from his long drive from Los Angeles. He pulled the curtain closed. From his last unpacked bag, he removed a laptop and printer. Placing the laptop precisely in the middle of the desk and the printer exactly a foot to the right, he inserted the power cords, plugged the other ends into the wall, and watched as the screen and power buttons lit up.

Bringing up the word processing program, he opened a new page and typed.

TERRORIST

No. Too bland. Everybody is a terrorist these days. He deleted the word.

ECO-TERRORIST

No. Too politically correct. Besides, he didn't give a flip about the environment. In fact, there wasn't going to be a lot of environment left when he was done. He deleted that too.

EXTREMIST

No. It didn't convey whether it was for the good or for the bad. Another deletion.

The man wanted a good descriptor. He needed headlines as fast as possible, with as many newspapers using his name as possible. His public name needed to be short, strong, and definite but have the taste of surprise, something mysterious, and a ring of cleverness that would be memorable. He wanted to be called something that the media idiots would analyze to see if they could tell his intentions by dissecting his name.

The man laughed. They were fools. His major concern was that he have a name that fit well into a headline.

He'd decided he would need a two-part name: a first name, which he would use over and over so people could connect him to every action, and a second name, which would convey a broader category of identity, a title, a recognition of his role in whatever havoc he would wreak. The second name would change for each action.

His full name, the one he would use in all public interactions, would be the sum of the first plus the second.

His first name would tell people *who* he was, the second would tell *what* he was.

Looking at business cards had given him the idea. A name and a title. Using a two-part moniker for a hero was different, but not unusual. Many of his heroes had names and titles, like Magneto, Savior of Mutants, and General Zod, Nemesis of Jorel.

The decision on his second name, his title, wouldn't be made until he had decided on a particular action. It would then be chosen to reflect the location or even something historical about the place. The media always appreciated a descriptor that connected to something familiar.

Last year, he'd decided on his first name. He never even told his cellmate, which was a good thing because it would have gotten around and become a joke. His first name was simple and direct: Dr. Death.

Straightforward, good cadence, right to the point, but mysterious.

It was *who* he is.

All he needed now was the *what*.

PSYCHOPATH

No. Everybody's a psychopath, even if they don't know it. And they'd use that label anyway. Delete.

THE EVIL ONE

Hmm. Not bad. But was it surprising? Delete.

CROOK

That would be funny, so it wouldn't work. He'd look like an amateur. Delete.

OUTLAW

He paused, rewrote it, and then wrote it again.

OUTLAW

OUTLAW

OUTLAW

OUTLAW

He liked it. It had a western flavor to it, like the movies he had watched as a kid. And his first action would definitely be connected to the West, so it fit perfectly. Wasn't there a TV special he had seen once, something about outlaws in the West?

Butch Cassidy. That was it. *Butch Cassidy and the Sundance Kid.* It was really good, and the characters were easy to remember. They were outlaws, but their brand of hate was reserved for the rich and powerful.

He liked it.

The man searched through the folders in his third bag for the business card form. He inserted a sheet into the printer and launched the application.

No need to shout or be loud, simple and straightforward would do.

Breathe. Relax. Focus.

A few keystrokes, a whir, a *thuck* when the paper hit the output tray.

He tore apart the perforations, made a neat stack of the cards on the desk, and then held up the first one:

DR. DEATH, OUTLAW

Who he is, what he is.

He really liked it.

Within a few days, every newspaper in the country would have his name on the front page.

CHAPTER 5

"**W**oohoo!"

Mogi launched himself into a flying leap from the McDowells' houseboat to the dock and then sprinted toward the marina parking lot.

Jennifer, startled by the whoop, watched as her brother raced down the pier. "Oh, good grief," she said under her breath. "What's he done, now?"

She arrived at the parking area in time to see Jefferson, a friend from school, helping Mogi pull some bulky duffel bags from the trunk of Jefferson's car.

Mogi opened the bags and quickly laid out two air tanks, harnesses, respirators, weight belts, fins, masks, emergency inflation vests, assorted gauges, and other items of diving equipment.

Tossing the empty bags to the side, he danced an excited jig around the equipment.

"Where in the world did you get that?" she asked.

"Craigslist. Some guy moved to Flagstaff from California and was selling all of his and his wife's diving stuff. I bet I got it for half-price or less!"

"I bet half-price was still a good chunk of money. Where you'd get it?"

"Remember last year when the school hired me to cut down all the weeds around the buildings? I put it with my Christmas money and had just enough."

"Do Mom and Dad know about this?"

"Well, not yet, but I timed it so everything would come after we'd gotten our certification, so it shouldn't be a big surprise. I mean, they should expect it, right? I used the credit card they gave us for emergencies—I'll pay them back when I get home."

"Mogi, you—" Jennifer began to scold.

"And, no doubt you've noticed that I got you a set, too?"

That really made it hard for her to rag on him, but she gave it her best. Truth was, after having earned her own certification, Jennifer was as excited as her brother at having her own equipment. That made sorting through the equipment on the pavement the high point of the day for both brother and sister. But after they and Jefferson carried it all back to the houseboat, it was back to work.

The McDowell houseboat wasn't big, or new, or as fancy as most of the rental houseboats. And it wasn't as pretty, or clean, or as cool.

Well, actually, Jennifer admitted, it was really old and pretty, well, trashed.

The McDowells had hosted plenty of friends over

the years, and the small houseboat now showcased every spill, tear, and scratch—decades of use and abuse—it had ever been subjected to. And no matter what Mogi did to fix it, the air conditioner only wheezed out streams of hot air.

The materials had been brought the weekend before.

In exchange for using the houseboat, Mogi and Jennifer would paint the doors and railings, scrub the vinyl floors, hang new curtains, replace the bedding, and refresh the old sofa cushions with new filling and slipcovers. They'd clean the bathroom, wash the windows, and reline the kitchen drawers and shelves. The last effort would be to replace the fake grass outdoor carpet on the upper deck.

"We've got plenty of time," Mogi had told his sister when they first arrived. "This is all simple stuff. It will be a piece of cake."

But Jennifer had found that she was spending an hour or more working every night, marking things off the to-do list, while Mogi spent his evenings in the upper deck's lounge chair, playing games on his iPad. Apparently, the piece of cake he had referred to was *his* piece of the cake, not hers.

She'd finally had enough.

"Up! Get up!" she'd shouted as she pulled the earphones out of his ears. "I'm not doing this all by myself, and I'm not about to be stuck finishing everything on the Fourth."

Mogi had admitted his guilt, bought a little forgiveness by promising to fix hamburgers for dinner, and then sincerely decided that maybe he needed to get with the program. He had joined her in doing whatever was next on the list, and on the day after the class ended, he painted the doors. By the time Jefferson had arrived with the equipment, he had even finished painting the rails. That took care of everything but the replacement of the fake grass on the top deck.

They started on a corner of the upper deck, tugging at whatever edges they could liberate from the years-old paste.

Mogi used a pair of pliers to hold the old covering as Jennifer shoved a stiff putty knife under the carpet to pry the surfaces apart. It was much harder than they had expected, and both were soaked with sweat before it was finished.

When they had managed to strip off the last piece, the whole surface of the deck was sticky with the old glue, making it impossible to walk on. In the heat of the late afternoon, each of them took a putty knife and scraped the semi-melted residue from one side of the deck to the other.

"I have an idea," Mogi said during a break in the shade of the upper deck's canopy. "Let's finish scraping, then call it a day. We'll get the tools back into the toolboxes, haul the old carpet and trash to the dumpster, and then drive the houseboat around to where we did our class. We'll get the new carpet laid out and cut early in the morning, then glue it down tomorrow night, when it's cooler. We'll be done before the weekend even starts."

"And that," Jennifer pointed out, "would give us the afternoon to try out our new equipment. I bet you didn't think about that."

Mogi just smiled.

It took three hours to finish with the old glue, straighten up the cabin, haul away the trash, buy groceries, get more water, retrieve the air tanks they had left at the marina for filling, gas up both the houseboat and the small speedboat that it pulled behind, and putter out of Hite Marina into the center of the upper lake.

Forty-five minutes later, they pulled into a good anchorage in White Canyon Bay. Mogi had suggested Farley Canyon Bay, since they knew it better from their class, but Jennifer liked White Canyon better. It was relatively new territory, and the bay went farther up into the foothills. That meant shallower water and more dramatic underwater features.

—————

It was noon the next day before they finished cutting the new carpet, leaving both of them exhausted from the heat. Fitting it around each railing upright took far more time than expected. With the sun directly overhead, the two finally called it quits. It was time to play.

Though he had been anxious and in a hurry during the class, Mogi was now slow and cautious as he and Jennifer prepared their equipment. They inspected each piece of gear, tried the regulators and tanks before they got in the water, and went over the safety list from memory. He was particularly concerned that they got the weight belts correct and made absolutely sure they both put on the emergency flotation vests.

One at a time, they geared up, pulled their fins on, stepped awkwardly down the old ladder next to the engines, and pushed off into the water. Mogi gave a thumbs-up and turned to follow the shoreline, trying not to grin too much with the regulator in his mouth.

They stayed side by side, keeping close to the shore, moving in and out as the rock shelf varied in width.

Several massive boulders provided entertainment as the brother and sister went down, up, around, over, below, above, and every which way to enjoy their newfound weightlessness. They also played a salvage game, each trying to find the most entertaining item on the lake floor that had been lost overboard by houseboats and speedboats.

Against the repeating gurgle of his respirator, Mogi heard a new sound. It was a muffled whir. Looking into the darkness of the deeper water, he saw a faint, metallic object slowly materialize.

The funny-looking fish was back.

Signaling Jennifer to hover behind a boulder, they peeked around to watch the fish as it came closer.

It only took a moment before Mogi realized that it had to be a submarine.

Kind of.

It wasn't the big, sleek, monstrous machines of the

military nor the high-tech, glass-plated mini-subs seen in James Bond movies. The object, as it passed by, looked more like a miniature junkyard version from a high school science experiment. It had a misshapen center capsule with two long cylindrical tubes on each side, two propellers, and a strange-looking oblong window on top, lit with a soft light bright enough to show the pilot inside.

Extending from the front were long mechanical arms, like on robots. Lights were mounted above the arms.

It looked like a submarine one might find at a garage sale.

The awkward object floated by, slowed, did a 360, stopped, and hung silently above them in the muddled splotches of sunlight filtering from above.

Mogi realized that the man inside, wearing a puzzled look, was watching two streams of bubbles rise up from a mud-covered boulder on the canyon shelf. It took a couple of seconds before he followed the bubbles down to the air tanks of two wide-eyed divers.

He was clearly startled to see them, mouthed something to himself, and then maneuvered the silvery fish to swing around in the water and plummet back into the darkness.

CHAPTER 6

ogi and Jennifer were stunned. What in the world was a submarine doing in Lake Powell?

"Are you even allowed to have a submarine in Lake Powell?" Jennifer asked as she joined her brother in the shade of the top deck, handing him a soda. They had returned to the McDowells' boat, leaving enough air in their tanks for another dive later.

"You got me," Mogi replied. "I don't remember seeing anything that said you couldn't. But I haven't seen it posted that you couldn't have an aircraft carrier, either."

Mogi kept an eye on the odd, little houseboat across the bay—the one covered with solar panels. It had to be related to the mysterious submarine since they looked like they'd both come from the same garage sale. He remembered the man's face as he and the other students were ferried back to the marina. The two faces—in the deep of Farley Canyon Bay and in the houseboat's window—had been the same, and now he had seen it a third time.

Across the bay, the backdoor of the houseboat opened and a man appeared. He pulled the fishing boat close to the deck, got in, started the motor, backed out, and headed across the bay, directly toward Mogi and Jennifer.

The siblings looked at each other wide-eyed.

When the small boat pulled up to their stern, Mogi was waiting to tie up the bow line and help the man aboard.

Stocky, medium height, slightly bald, and with a short, white beard, the man certainly appeared to pose no danger. The three exchanged greetings and went up the ladder to the top deck, where the man graciously accepted a lawn chair and a cold drink.

"Unless I'm mistaken," he said once he was settled in his chair, "we've met before."

Mogi and Jennifer both replied with guilty looks.

"Well, I felt I should introduce myself and confess that you've caught me in a rather delicate situation. If the authorities were to discover my little secret, I'm sure that someone would feel the need to expose my activities. So, I'm more or less here to ask for your silence.

"My name is Nigel Hawthorne. I'm an engineering professor at the University of Utah in Salt Lake City. I'm also a history buff. I've made it my hobby to discover stories about the lesser-known characters in history, especially if they're associated with Utah."

Mogi couldn't contain himself anymore. "Is the

submarine yours? Did you build it? How did you get it to the lake? What are you doing with it? What's it like inside?"

Hawthorne laughed. "You have a lot of questions, I'm sure, and I promise to answer all of them in due time. I will even give you a tour, if you'd like. But, to begin with, it is indeed my submarine. I built it, and I'm using it to do research. If you'll give me a chance to explain what I'm using it for, it might draw a better picture of why I built it and why it's necessary that its, um, existence, shall we say, remain under the radar from our government."

He took a long drink from his glass and leaned forward.

"I'm chasing an outlaw named Butch Cassidy."

The professor told the story of Robert LeRoy Parker, born on Friday the thirteenth, April 1866. He spent his early life in the tiny town of Circleville, Utah, not more than a couple of hours northwest of where the McDowells' houseboat currently floated in the water.

His first home was a two-room log cabin. It was a happy home, but the family was desperately poor, and Robert grew up working any job to help the family out.

He had natural talents for training and riding horses, he understood the business of cattle ranching, he knew how to use guns, and he possessed a gentle, easy-going, happy nature. People liked him.

He left home in 1884. Taking various names, which was not unusual for the times, he eventually adopted *Butch Cassidy*—the last name from a friend he admired, and the first from a brief job he had as a butcher.

"There's little doubt that he was a good man," Hawthorne said. "People gravitated to him wherever he went. He was honest, straightforward, and easy to get along with—a fast talker and a good companion. He was also handsome, with piercing blue eyes.

"For the first few years away from home, he worked ranches throughout Utah, Wyoming, Colorado, Montana, and even into Nebraska, making a name for himself as a hard worker. But, for whatever reason, he just wasn't the settling-down type of person.

"He also seemed drawn to people on the wrong side of the law. Eventually, he was accused and convicted of several things, most of which he hadn't done, like stealing saddles, horses, or cattle, and spent a year in the Wyoming Penitentiary, which is where he met more of the bad crowd. He had always been a fast learner, and it wasn't long before he became well-schooled in ways of making a living that were far easier than being a cowboy.

"In 1889, after being released from prison, he robbed his first bank in Telluride, Colorado."

The professor stood and began pacing across the deck, much like he was in a classroom giving a lecture.

"If you want the full story, you'd be best off by reading some of the excellent books written about him. The major points I want to make are that he was basically a good man and a good friend, and he was smart. He was probably the smartest outlaw of his time. Butch figured out that after robbing a bank, or a train, or a mine payroll office, a sheriff's posse would usually be organized on the spur of the moment and would quickly set out to catch whoever did it. This meant that most of the just-recruited people and their horses were unprepared to go very far, or very fast, or very long.

"Butch figured that if a band of outlaws could ride long enough and far enough immediately after their crime, the lawmen and their posses would almost always give up along the way. With that in mind, he organized a network of hideouts, camps, and ranches where he could store food, water, and fresh horses. Being personable to begin with, he made friends with ranchers all over the countryside and had them provide whatever he needed when he was running from the law.

"Every few months, he and his gang would rob a train, hold up a bank, or whatever, and then separate, each member of the gang riding in a different direction, using different parts of the network to make their escape. Swapping for fresh horses, food, and supplies along the way, they'd ride far and fast all over the country. Some days later, the gang members would meet at one place to divide up the loot. Afterward, they'd continue to ride hundreds of miles away as fast as they could.

"We have a story of Butch robbing a train in the middle of Wyoming and being more than a thousand miles away in New Mexico a few days later. That was not unusual. The posse after them would wear out, get lost, or essentially starve while trying to keep up."

"No one ever turned him in?" Jennifer asked.

"There were occasions when people were forced to reveal the whereabouts of the outlaws," the professor replied, "but it was uncommon. He made loyal friends. Of course, he paid them for their loyalty. That was one rule he did not break. He understood the importance of helping those who helped him, so he would often pay them in advance for their help. He also stole only from what he considered rich people—banks and railroads, mainly. The general populace didn't have a very high opinion of those people, so if they could help Butch, it was a good deed in their minds.

"Okay, where was I? Oh, yes. Butch had three major hideouts, each specifically chosen because they were hard to find, easy to defend, and had lots of space for lots of outlaws. These hideouts were so well known that the paths between them became known as the Outlaw Trail. His most well-hidden is an hour of so north of here, called Robbers' Roost.

"What's important," Hawthorne continued, "is that Butch was smart. Knowing that groups of people were easier to find, he didn't keep his gang together. He published coded messages in the personal columns of newspapers in different towns, using those messages to keep everybody informed of what was going on, setting new places to meet, or advising them to stay out of sight for a while.

"In addition, since some of the gang members might not know the way to the different meeting places, Butch used secret marks to guide his men through rough and confusing country. His marks didn't look like marks at all, if you didn't know what you were looking at. But if you did, you would know that you were on the right trail."

The professor paused to take in the mellowing light of the sunset.

"In particular," he continued, walking over to the railing, "there is some evidence that he put a secret mark on the wall of a canyon that was one of the most important trails in southern Utah."

He pointed to the entrance of White Canyon Bay.

"Right out there, about two hundred feet under the water."

The professor turned and looked at Mogi and Jennifer.

"I'm using the sub to look for it."

CHAPTER 7

D r. Death gazed out the hotel window at the evening life of the marina. He had returned his computer and printer to the bag and then moved the desk and chair back to their original places. With the room dark, assuring that he couldn't be seen, he watched the myriad of lights bobbing on the immense bay below him.

The Wahweap Marina and Lodge were on the south end of the lake, as opposed to Hite Marina, which was on the north end. It was the largest complex on Lake Powell, only a couple of miles west of Glen Canyon Dam. The marina itself was several football fields in length along the shore of the lake, with several long docks to accommodate the dozens of personal and rental houseboats, a separate dock for supplies and gas, and shorter docks for small boats. The three-story lodge, a restaurant and gift shop, and a large administration building were spread out along a rise above the marina.

The man enjoyed the sparkling lights of the evening: the long strings of bulbs along each dock, the dancing lights on the small boats coming and going across the bay, and the lights of the various shops.

It had been a long time.

Twelve years. He had looked at his cell walls every day for twelve years. How many times had he walked the eight steps from the cell door to the opposite wall and then walked the eight steps back?

He had almost gone insane. Many thought he had, which was fine with him—they left the crazies alone.

The cramped quarters, the constant noise of people mouthing off to one another, the constant clank of metal doors being opened and shut, the screeching of the metal chairs dragged across the cement floor in the day room, the constant feeling of uselessness hanging in the air—it was all a cesspool. Once you got sucked in, it coated your body with a never-ending assortment of foulness. If you stayed too long in the cesspool, you became the foulness.

He was on the verge of being sucked in when he stumbled onto his salvation.

The secret was in the pages of his comics.

Other people thought of them only as cartoons. But when the man looked at them—studied them, memorized them—he saw the raw power, the pure strength, the sensational personalities. Those heroes inside the pages lived in a world vastly superior to his, and they began to speak to him, to call to him, to whisper to him. They invited him into their world.

That world could be his, they said, if he would only join them.

Slowly grasping the truth within the graphic covers, he gathered more of the precious documents. It took careful planning on his part and years for the materials to fall into place. By being disciplined with his money, researching his purchases, and carefully protecting his materials from others, he acquired all the comics he needed to access their world.

When he had discovered their world and made it his, when he had finally yielded all that he was, and when he had accepted all that they offered, he not only inherited their world but had been given a destiny.

Now he was out. There was nothing to prevent him from achieving his destiny. The man smiled, took a deep breath, and exulted in his freedom.

He took a clean sheet from his luggage, spread it out on the floor, and smoothed the wrinkles. Next, he took his stacks of comic books from the bed and placed them strategically along each edge of the sheet, leaving room down the center. Then he removed his clothes and lay naked between the stacks, carefully aligned so that each stack was within reach of his fingers.

Closing his eyes, he concentrated on his breathing and his heart rate.

Breathe. Relax. Focus.

Gradually, he rose up, slid a comic off a stack, and laid it against his feet. Another one followed.

Lex Luthor, Kingpin, Professor Zoom, Ra's Al Ghul.

He focused on their names, silently mouthing each name, their enemies' names, the battles they had fought, and the victories they had earned. He slid more magazines across his legs and feet, against his knees, along his thighs.

Two-Face, Violator, Loki, Bane.

He remembered the distinctive powers they possessed, the wondrous ways they laid waste to the unprotected, the way they used their unique powers to destroy the forces of good, and the depth of their abilities to create extraordinary hardships for nations, the world, and the universe.

His heroes judged the world and rendered punishment.

Magneto, the Lizard, Harley Quinn, Kraven.

Rippling muscles, obscured faces, haunting voices dripping with evil. And the grins—the in-your-face attitudes that reeked of dominance and unashamed superiority—the grins reflected their indomitable spirits.

They were magnificent!

He reverently slid each comic over his body— across his midsection, up his chest, under his chin, around his head. He bathed in the memories of the stories.

Norman Osborn, Poison Ivy, Sebastian Shaw, Scarecrow.

Breathing slower and deeper, Dr. Death, Outlaw, lay covered with the epic lives of his heroes and their villains. His mind swam in their conflicts, their challenges, and their struggles between good and evil. He felt the muscles, the strains, the fears, the gleeful moments, the one-on-one matches with superbly crafted opponents, and shuddered with the strength of his heroes' common identity with the world of evil.

They were family.

It was a far cry from the family he had grown up with—his parents, with their screaming and shouting and beatings, and then the string of foster families, all of whom were loving and devoted in the beginning but turned hateful and disgusted when he refused their superficial emotions and juvenile punishments. They proclaimed goodness, but he saw through them: It was dominance and obedience that they really wanted, not virtue. They wanted him to be just like them and could not accept his uniqueness.

One by one, he rejected those false families and their false affections until he found his *real* family, the family that exposed the pathetic, so-called righteousness of the world and embraced the true source of honor and the way of the warrior. He did not have superpowers, he was not from another planet, and he did not have an opponent equivalent to those heroes of dark powers, but it was to that family that he truly belonged.

His heroes were the lights that had brought him out of darkness. And now his time had come to openly declare himself a member of that family. He was ready to step forward, to reveal himself, to accept the role that he was expected to play.

The time had come for him to accomplish evil. It was his destiny.

Breathe. Relax. Focus.

The man allowed himself to sleep, to complete his ritual cleansing. When he awoke in the morning, he would be in harmony with himself, composed in the power of unity. He would move in the ordinary world, but he would be of the other world.

With the light of dawn coming through the window, the man calling himself Dr. Death, Outlaw, woke up, took a shower, dressed in clean clothes, returned his comics to the large bag, and then packed his belongings.

He took his bags to the van, returned to straighten his room, and then stood in reverent silence in front of the window, thinking about what he was about to do.

The vision had come to him before he was released from prison. Working with his early concepts, reading and memorizing maps, exploring the requirements for his actions, he carefully filled in the details. In the end, he was confident that everything would come together. He was excited and confident.

He was going to blow up Glen Canyon Dam.

CHAPTER 8

It would be an unimaginable catastrophe. Glen Canyon Dam held back enough water that, if suddenly released, every dam and bridge across the river for hundreds of miles downstream would be ripped from its foundations. The cities along the way would be scoured from the land, the canals and aqueducts would be flushed from the landscape, highways would be torn apart. Without water for any length of time, the crops of Southern California would cook dead in the sun, and the loss of electricity would leave Los Angeles in the dark for years. Millions could die.

It left him breathless just thinking about it.

It was a very good choice. It would get people's attention. He'd be in the newspapers for weeks. He'd be written into history books! Not his real name, of course. They would never know his real name. They would only know his hero name: DR. DEATH, OUTLAW.

The man stood at the window, remembering all

the careful planning he had done and how he had dreamed of the awesome destruction that would come from his actions.

And then he remembered how it had all fallen apart.

The original method of blowing up the dam was sound, he thought: a surplus Navy torpedo secretly attached under a houseboat. Aimed straight at the dam, the torpedo would be launched down the lake to slam into the massive concrete structure. With the force of the explosive, the momentum of the torpedo, and the pressure of the water, the dam would split in half and then crumble like a clod of dirt in water.

His weapons supplier laughed at the idea, which irritated him, but he finally accepted that the guy was right.

It was a simple and elegant solution, but a four-thousand-pound, nineteen-foot-long torpedo would be a little difficult to hook onto the bottom of a houseboat without being noticed.

So he had developed a new plan. He would stash a large amount of explosives on a houseboat and send it by remote control to crash into the dam.

His supplier said that idea wouldn't work either. An explosion only on the surface of the concrete dam, at the surface of the water and without any penetration, wouldn't do enough damage to make the dam collapse.

It would be, simply put, a noisy flop.

Okay, okay. So he would drop lots of explosives overboard at the base of the dam and let them sink to the bottom before being detonated. It would crack the bedrock at the bottom of the dam and cause the whole thing to collapse.

That didn't impress his supplier either—aerial photos on Google showed a chained-off area of the lake in front of the dam. He'd never get the boat close enough.

Then he asked if a miniature submarine was available.

Oh, that got a lot of laughs, which irritated him even more.

His next plan was to drop explosives from the cliffs above the dam, but the tops of the cliffs were also in restricted areas.

The next iteration of the plan involved blowing up enough explosives in the center of the lake to cause a huge wave to slam into the dam, causing it to crack down the middle. A homemade tsunami.

Unfortunately, after his supplier did the calculations, he learned that the amount of explosives needed to generate a wave big enough was a lot more than he expected—like a hundred tons or something —and it would take a ship the size of the Washington Monument to carry them. Okay, forget that one.

After a while, as surefire as each of his ideas had seemed, the man understood that it was time for a little honesty: He was not going to blow up the dam. He felt that he was really, really, really close, but he just didn't have enough of his ducks in a row. He'd have to devastate the nation another day.

Dr. Death, of course, was disappointed. The man

had thought about the dam's destruction for so long that it was hard to give up his dreams, but his cleansings helped him to steady his mind and to finally accept his limitations. Even the Great Ones knew to bide their time and pick their battles.

The truth brought his next decision: He'd make this a practice run. It would be a chance to rehearse his performance, to learn to be practical about his plans, and to establish some of his tools and processes —the decision about his name, the business cards, the payment method for the stuff he needed, his procedures for acquiring materials, working out his transportation, testing his escape plans, his approach to advertising and marketing, and so on.

Besides, he had already bought the explosives—his supplier had offered him a Fourth of July holiday discount—and he'd sent in his deposit for renting a houseboat months ago. If he couldn't do the dam, there had to be something else at the lake that he could destroy.

Dr. Death spent a week reviewing maps of the lake for a target that would be possible. He needed a small, well-placed, clean act of destruction that would increase his confidence, sharpen his skills, and build his self-esteem.

Practice makes perfect, people always said.

He settled on the Highway 95 bridge at the other end of the lake. The highway crossing the bridge connected the area on the east side of the lake with the area on the west side. It took some negotiating to trade the reservation for a houseboat at the southernmost marina for a houseboat at the northernmost marina, especially on the Fourth of July weekend, but he was lucky—there was a recent cancelation at Hite Marina, and he quickly traded one houseboat for the other.

The Highway 95 bridge went across the Colorado River as it flowed into the lake. The roadway was supported by two long, continuous arches of steel, one on each side of the roadway, bent gracefully up from below the road on one side, over and down to the other side.

The ends of the two arches were firmly anchored in concrete piers the size of small buildings.

Dr. Death would not have to blow up the bridge.

He would only need to blow up the canyon wall that held one of the concrete piers. The weight of the bridge itself would cause the pier to give way, twisting the steel of the arch, pulling the roadway from the canyon walls, and sending it into the river. He wasn't sure of the total effect of the damage or level of hurt it would cause, but it would certainly be inconvenient to people. He was sorry that maybe not even a single person would actually die, but maybe someone would be unlucky enough to be on the bridge when it collapsed. You never know.

Ah, well. Simple, clean, well-done, good press, good escape. Good practice. It would be a warning shot to let everybody know that greater things were coming. He'd scatter some business cards around to make sure he got credit, but save the bigger publicity for later. You have to crawl before you can walk, he told himself.

It was time to get going. His destiny awaited him. And he might stop for breakfast, he was pretty hungry.

The man opened the door and carefully checked the hallway. Finding it empty, he acted casual as he walked to the panel van he had rented in Los Angeles. In the back were ten large coolers, stacked two high and carefully tied down. Each cooler was crammed with explosives. Behind the passenger seat were two duffel bags of diving equipment and his personal bags, and in a suitcase in front were the timing gear, detonators, wires, and tools.

He headed east, crossing over the dam he so passionately wanted to destroy. Hite Marina, where his newly rented houseboat was located, was at the end of a long drive north.

I'll be back, he promised himself. The original idea was too sweet to let go.

It would take a long day of driving from the south end of the lake to the north, heading east across the top of Arizona, through Kayenta, and then turning north through Mexican Hat, Utah. A hundred miles after that, he would turn onto Highway 95 and head back toward Lake Powell. He'd turn off for the Hite Marina only a few miles before the Highway 95 bridge crossed over the Colorado River.

Reviewing the map of the lake, Dr. Death confirmed to himself that he had made an excellent choice.

Officially, the Highway 95 bridge went over the river where the lake started. In fact, a picture of the bridge included on the map clearly showed that the lake actually backed up into the river's channel a mile or two above the bridge.

That meant he could drive a motorboat completely under the bridge. All he had to do was put the explosives in a half-circle below the pier and set a timer. When it went off, he'd be a mile down the lake, sitting easy in his speedboat, watching the bridge come down.

Simple, straightforward. Nice and easy.

That took care of the planning. The only thing left was finding an out-of-the-way place to anchor the houseboat, which would be his command center. He'd live on the houseboat and run the speedboat back and forth to the bridge to set things up. Sweet! He'd seen the picture of the houseboat and it was going to be a palace compared to the hotel room.

Dr. Death looked at the lake map as he negotiated the highway to the Hite Marina turn-off. He saw a long, narrow canyon that would suit his needs.

White Canyon Bay.

Perfect, he told himself. I probably won't run into another person.

CHAPTER 9

Grabbing the railing of the solar panel-laden houseboat, Mogi placed his foot on the deck and stepped over.

He moved around the outboard motor and squeezed under a solar panel, allowing more room for Hawthorne and Jennifer to step onto the deck behind him. Leaving his old fishing boat tied to the stern, the professor scooted around his two visitors and unlocked the stout cabin door. He flipped several switches on the inside wall and moved through the door onto a walkway.

The walkway circled the inside of the outer walls of the cabin. The rest of the floor, where the bedrooms, kitchen, and living room should have been, had been removed, and a hole was cut into the floor—a big, rectangular hole the size of a medium-sized swimming pool.

In that big opening, gently rocking in the water, was the dorkiest-looking object Mogi had ever seen.

"I'll let you look for a minute, then I'll explain," the professor said.

Mogi and Jennifer stared. Their brief glimpse of the submarine beneath the water hadn't come close to showing how strange the thing really was. It was an awkward, asymmetrical object, metal in most places but oddly colored where it was painted at all. A lopsided glass-and-metal cover to the submarine stood open at an angle.

Mogi finally realized what they were looking at.

"It was called an F-100 SuperSabre, a jet fighter commonly used in the Vietnam War era," the professor said.

"A group of restoration buffs rebuilt this one for a traveling air show. Unfortunately, it was caught in a storm while in a hangar, and a roof beam fell across it just behind the cockpit, destroying the engine and cutting the plane in half. I was able to buy the whole front half. The back half went to a salvage yard."

The submarine was made of the cockpit, where the pilot sat, plus the nose in front and a little of the original fuselage behind. About sixteen feet long, the nose of the jet looked whole, while the portion behind the cockpit was covered by welded plates. The window was the original, thick, dome-shaped canopy, held open by the powerful lifting mechanism that pilots used to get in and out of the plane.

Along each side of the cockpit was a long, smooth cylinder connected by a metal pipe, like the outriggers on a canoe. Various other tubes, pipes, cables, and lights were attached haphazardly around the center section. A couple of folded mechanical arms were attached at the front of the nose.

Two keg-shaped motors with propellers were mounted to the top and bottom of the welded wall behind the cockpit. Mogi recognized them as scuba self-propulsion systems—personal, battery-driven motors with propellers that scuba divers held in front of themselves to be whisked along underwater. Cables from inside the cockpit controlled their directions.

The cockpit itself appeared well made, but the metal patches were crooked, the holes where the wings of the plane had been were welded over with plates that had obviously been hammered into place, the hole from where the front wheel operated was welded closed with irregular metal plates, the struts that attached the large cylinders to the sides were irregular and bent, and any attempts at painting must have involved a smattering of leftover paint cans.

It was no work of art. That was for sure.

Mogi edged around the walkway, from one side of the houseboat to the other, looking closely at the object floating in the water.

"It's obvious that my skills as an engineer are on the theoretical side," the professor said. "What can I say? I'm a lousy welder. However, I would like to take credit for the fact that everything is watertight and that the sub actually works.

"The cockpit, obviously, is where I sit. The cylinders on the sides are my ballast tanks. When I pump air into the tanks, the sub goes up. When I pump water in, it sinks.

"The propellers get me going forward and backward, and I change the way they point by rotating the control handle, so that gives me steering. And I have an air balancing system inside the cockpit that uses air tanks to keep the cockpit's air pressure constant, no matter how deep I dive.

"The biggest concern, of course, is having juice in the batteries. I have an hour's worth of charge, maximum. If I lose charge, I'm just a piece of junk suspended in the water. I have an emergency dive tank and respirator beside me in case I ever get into trouble. But if I had to open the canopy to get out, the cockpit would fill with water and the sub would sink straight to the bottom of the lake."

"That's why there are so many solar panels on the houseboat," Mogi interrupted, realizing the answer to one of his questions. "You use them to charge the batteries."

"Oh, yes," the professor said. "The pumps are electric, the propulsion system is electric, and the manipulator arms are electric. And, of course, the lights."

Hawthorne pointed through the open canopy to the space below the cockpit's seat. "The batteries are all stored along the bottom of the cockpit—I call it the first level—while I sit in the second level, with the seat, control cables, pumps, switches, and everything else."

"Is that the original seat from the jet?" Mogi asked, peering closely.

"Yes, the very one the pilots used," the professor replied. "I was going to take it out to save on weight, but after sitting in it, I just couldn't. It feels too good. I did remove the parachute that was built into the seat, but everything else exists just as it was restored. Go ahead if you'd like. Climb in."

Mogi gingerly stepped on the ballast tank, tested it, and then knelt as he swung a leg through the cockpit opening and onto the seat. Steadying himself, he brought his other leg over and sat down.

Wow.

Mogi understood the professor's comment. Sitting in the pilot's seat was like sitting on a throne.

He looked at the controls in front of him. Along the left side were several gauges on an added metal plate, and a similar plate on the right side held knobs, switches, and a regular motorboat throttle. Along the top were the handles to the long manipulator arms in front. In the middle, hinged to the floor, with a handle just above the height of his knees, was the control stick.

"I disconnected the aircraft controls," Hawthorne explained, kneeling down closer to the sub. "You can't see it, but I've got a waterproof digital control box under the dash that uses a microprocessor to control the ballast tanks and the motors. Everything is hooked to the control stick, so if I want to go up, I pull on the stick. If I want to go down, I push on the stick. I move the stick to the side when I want to turn. The boat throttle controls the speed of the motors, forward and backward."

While Mogi read the labels above the switches and knobs and gently moved the control stick around, imagining himself operating the sub, Jennifer was looking at the inside of the cabin.

The walls were covered with photographs, diagrams, labels, articles, drawings, and maps. One portion of the wall had a series of photographs taped together, making a panorama. She peeked into the front of the houseboat—where two rooms had been preserved as a bathroom and bedroom—their walls were also covered with taped-up sheets of paper. A chair, desk, computer, and printer were crammed in beside the mattress on the floor of the bedroom. Books were stacked in various piles around the floor.

It was a mess.

Butch Cassidy was the obvious topic across the papers, though there must have been a hundred photographs of wall carvings, Indian petroglyphs, pictographs, and obscure markings. Several articles were about a man named William T. Phillips, and other pages were copied from different books about robbers, outlaws, crooks, and Utah history.

The professor signaled for the attention of the two teens. He pulled a folding chair out of a corner and retrieved the desk chair from his bedroom. Mogi got out of the sub and joined his sister as they sat down.

"I believe that Butch Cassidy put a mark on a rock wall someplace below us," the professor said, "to indicate that this canyon had the trail leading out of the river basin. He may have put the mark farther out, toward the center of the lake, where the entrance to

Farley Canyon is, or he may have put it in both places."

"What kind of mark are you looking for?" Jennifer asked.

"Well," the professor confessed, "that's part of the problem. I don't know what the mark looks like."

CHAPTER 10

Mogi looked surprised. "So how will you know it when you see it?" Hawthorne smiled. "Well, that requires a little bit more of the story. If you'll indulge me, I'll try to make this brief." The professor took on a more formal posture and continued the lecture he had started on the McDowells' houseboat.

"Butch Cassidy was famous for being smart, organized, fast, generous, and a creative robber of banks and trains. He was no Robin Hood, though. He gave generous pay-offs to those who helped his gang members along the trails, but he and his closest friend, Harry Longabaugh, the Sundance Kid, spent most of their money on card games, fancy clothes, good food, and expensive women."

"What they are best known for, however, was how they died."

The professor walked to a series of photographs on the wall. "At the beginning of the twentieth century, after years of robbing banks and trains, things were getting pretty hot for Butch and Sundance. Butch suddenly had this idea that they should move to South America. There was lots of land, rich grass, good water, and the prices for beef were high.

They could build a ranch and start new lives.

"So, in 1901, Butch, Sundance, and Sundance's girlfriend, a beautiful woman named Etta Place, moved to Argentina. Within a few years, they established a good ranch and were enjoying themselves. However, bad luck followed them.

"The Pinkerton Detective Agency was a famous firm hired to hunt down Butch and Sundance. Well, the agency never forgave Butch for not getting caught. When the Pinkertons learned of their ranch in Argentina, they sent detectives down to the area. In spite of the fact that Butch and Sundance had never committed a crime in Argentina, the detectives printed up WANTED posters and distributed them throughout the country. After a short time, Butch and Sundance were recognized. But, since the local officials and even the governor of the territory were friends with Butch, nothing much was made of it.

"Not long after, though, some robberies took place that had a certain flavor to them—mining payrolls were hit, banks were robbed—and the bandits used a network of ranches and hideouts to outrun their pursuers, much like Butch had created back in the states."

The professor looked sternly at Mogi and Jennifer.

"I think Butch and Sundance didn't have a thing to do with those robberies. Several of Butch's friends from America had followed them to Argentina and made themselves at home in the surrounding countryside. It was a nice, little community of semi-retired outlaws, and it was probably some of their friends who were now committing the robberies, using the methods that Butch had taught them.

"Well, the situation wasn't looking good, so Butch, Sundance, and Etta decided to leave their ranch and move on. Now, I mentioned that they liked living an expensive lifestyle. Since they no longer had the income from their ranch, money began to be a problem, and since they were getting blamed for the robberies anyway, it was natural that they go back to being outlaws. Stealing money was still a lot easier than working for it.

"From 1905 to around 1908, the team was back in business. At some point along the way, Etta returned to the United States and is never again mentioned in history. Butch and Sundance intended to steal just a little more money and then return to the US to join her.

"Sometime later, a mule train that carried the weekly payroll of a respected mining operation was robbed. Most of the witnesses agreed that the bandits were two well-armed white Americans. The descriptions matched Butch and Sundance. Two days after that, in a tiny Bolivian town named San Vicente, police killed two outlaws in a shootout. The two were not identified or recognized, but they were definitely gringos. It is assumed that those two men were the same men who robbed the mule train. The two bodies were buried in the local cemetery, with no headstones, and no names were ever recorded."

The professor paused to take a breath.

"Since Butch and Sundance were famous, some American magazines came to Bolivia to investigate. Interviews were done, evidence was gathered, newspaper and magazine articles were written, and history officially accepted that it was, indeed, Robert LeRoy Parker and Harry Longabaugh who lay at the bottom of those graves in that small, high Bolivian cemetery."

The professor sighed.

"In this case, however, one of them came back from the grave."

CHAPTER 11

Mogi and Jennifer followed Hawthorne as he pointed to a different set of papers further down the walkway.

"In 1925," he continued, "almost two decades after the killings in Bolivia, a new black Ford touring car pulled up in front of the old Parker ranch in Circleville, Utah. Now, remember that Circleville is where I started my story. It's where Butch was born and grew up.

"A man got out of the car and walked up to Mark Parker, one of the other twelve children of Butch's parents. The man looked familiar, and after exchanging pleasantries, Mark was absolutely convinced that it was his brother, Robert Parker, the outlaw known as Butch Cassidy. The long-lost brother had finally come home. The mysterious man met the other surviving members of the Parker family, including the father, and not one of them doubted that it was their brother or son.

"Over the next several years, more people reported seeing Butch—talking with him, playing a card game, or even putting him up for a night or two. He was seen at least a dozen times between 1908 and 1941. In almost every case, the witnesses were reliable people who should have known who they were talking to.

"But, and this is a big *but*, no one takes a picture, no one interviews him, and there is no information given about him that didn't already exist. That means there was no proof that it was Butch.

"Then, in the mid-1930s, something else happens. A manuscript of an unpublished book starts making the rounds to small publishers. The manuscript was written in 1934 by a man named William T. Phillips. Its title is *The Story of Butch Cassidy*, and it's a biography of the famous outlaw. But Phillips follows up the manuscript with the bold statement that it's not really a biography but an autobiography, and that he, William T. Phillips, is actually Butch Cassidy.

"Several friends believe him, and even some people who knew Butch believe him, but most people don't. Phillips's manuscript reveals nothing about Butch that wasn't already known. Phillips dies in 1937, and, without proof otherwise, history still believes that Butch Cassidy died in Bolivia."

He continued down the walkway, pointing at various papers, copies of newspapers, and photographs.

"In 2011, something extraordinary happens. A rare book dealer in Utah discovers an additional hundred pages of William T. Phillips's original manuscript. Unlike the manuscript in 1934, these pages reveal information that's never been heard before and, supposedly, information that nobody could have known other than Butch himself.

"Several Butch Cassidy experts immediately stood up and claimed that the newly found manuscript pages were a lot of bunk. They couldn't find anything of value. But, having read the extra pages, I found one sentence that could turn everybody on their heads."

He pointed to a sheet of paper taped to the wall with two sentences typed across it:

And I told him about my mark on the wall at White Canyon, so Harvey'd know the way. I told him to take the sacred oath after he was east of the river.

The professor's voice shrank to a whisper as he walked back toward them.

"In no other writing, book, article, letter, newspaper account, diary, interview, or court recording is there any mention of Butch putting a mark on the entrance to White Canyon. Only Butch would have known that it was done."

Hawthorne stood tall, his eyes shining.

"That, my good friends, is why I'm here. If I can find Butch's mark, I can prove that William T. Phillips had information that no one else had. That either makes him Butch Cassidy, as he claimed, or at least means that he talked to Butch Cassidy as the manuscript was being written.

"Either way, it would mean that Butch Cassidy did not die in Bolivia."

CHAPTER 12

"What do you think?" Jennifer asked Mogi that night as they sat on the McDowells' deck. The professor had brought them back after their two-hour visit. As they crossed the bay, they waved at a new houseboat motoring up the canyon. It looked just like the houseboat their dive class had used—new, long, and luxury equipped, with a shiny speedboat tied behind.

A small, thin, light-haired man at the helm waved back.

"Well," Mogi said, "you have to admit that this stuff is really interesting. Chasing little details about people is the kind of thing that history buffs live for."

"Did you look at his underwater pictures?" Jennifer asked. "He uses the sub to photograph the walls around the bottom of the cliffs and then puts all the pictures together in sequence, like a panorama. The entrance to White Canyon must include a quarter mile of formations along the riverbed. The entrance to Farley Canyon is part of the same area, so that's what the professor was doing when you saw him the first time."

"Did he find any marks on the walls?"

"Oh, yeah, lots, but they're obviously petroglyphs like what we see in the canyons back home. There must have been quite a community of ancient people up and down the Colorado River."

Mogi leaned back as he sipped his drink. "If White Canyon was the only trail out of the Colorado River basin, it must have been the major highway for everybody who lived in this country. How's the professor going to know a mark left by Butch Cassidy versus somebody else's mark?"

"It all depends on what the sentence in Phillips's manuscript means," Jennifer said. "While you were in the sub, he told me a little more. He said that the *Harvey* mentioned in the sentence was Harvey Logan, one of the longtime members of Cassidy's gang of outlaws.

"The professor believes that the Cassidy gang had robbed a train in Wyoming, and Harvey was riding to meet up with Butch. He ends up at Robbers' Roost, which is the hideout north of here. Harvey leaves the hideout, intending to meet Butch someplace in Colorado, but has to use White Canyon to get out of the basin. Having a mark at the entrance would let Harvey know which canyon was White Canyon. Without the mark, Harvey Logan would have wandered forever."

"The quote didn't say a whole lot," Mogi said.

"Well, I'm sure you remember it, but I took a picture with my phone anyway." She swished through a couple of screens, zoomed in, and read:

"And I told him about my mark on the wall at White Canyon, so Harvey'd know the way. I told him to take the sacred oath after he was east of the river."

"Does Dr. Hawthorne have any idea what *take the sacred oath* means?" Mogi asked.

"Nope."

"Well, I think he's doomed. With no idea of what the mark looks like, no idea of the location, and no idea what the quote means, he's got nothing. It might take years for him to photograph all the marks, or he might already have a picture of it and not know it. Without more information, I don't think he can figure this out."

———

Dr. Death couldn't have been more pleased.

He leaned back on the sofa in the living room of the houseboat, his legs stretched out, a beer in his hand. Eight steps forward, eight steps back. Now he had forty-nine steps, from the front of the houseboat to the outboard motors in the back.

He looked at the beer in his hand and knew it was a weakness. His body was a temple, he should not be polluting it. Soon, he would be through with this imperfection too.

It was all coming together.

He had struggled to retain his composure when he

signed the rental documents, but the driver's license he had bought back in LA worked fine. And the machine accepted the fake credit card too.

He had begun the action. His very first action.

His hands started shaking and he could feel his stomach clench.

Breathe. Relax. Focus.

Everything is fine. I left the motel. I dropped the envelope in the mail slot. I drove to the marina. I got the houseboat. I loaded the boxes. I had no problem driving the houseboat. I followed the map. And now I'm anchored.

No one checked me, no one patted me down, no one told me what to do, no one told me who to be. Nobody suspects a thing. Not a single person in the whole world knows who I am and where I am.

Breathe. Relax. Focus.

My time has come.

It is my destiny.

———

Alice Humbredt loved being a park ranger. She'd started five years before at the Saguaro National Park in Arizona, which wasn't exactly the top pick among rangers, but it was okay. Transferring to Lake Powell was a big step up, and she had fallen in love with the country.

Zooming around in the twin-engine, high-performance, super-fast, monster crook-catcher boat with the big red lights and siren was also awesome. Not that she got to do it much, but someday she'd get promoted out of her desk job and into the driver's seat. She couldn't wait. But until then, her role in the National Park Service was to handle this desk, and she would do it proudly.

The first order of the day was to sort the mail. She took a small envelope from the pile, slipped the opener under the flap, and gave it a quick flick.

A business card fell out. On one side was printed: *DR. DEATH, OUTLAW.*

On the opposite side of the card was written in ink: *THE FOURTH OF JULY.*

She held the card up, read it again, put it back in the envelope, and tossed it into the IN basket.

Great, she thought, another bozo for the holiday.

CHAPTER 13

Getting up at six o'clock in the morning was not Mogi's idea of fun. The fake grass carpet they'd laid out the night before had flattened across the area of the upper deck, making it easy for Mogi to square up the corners, straighten it against the metal edge of the deck, and get it fitted around the railing uprights. When he finished the cuts, he pulled the carpet's edge back two feet or so, used a paint roller to spread the glue, waited for it to become tacky, and then flopped the carpet back into place.

Jennifer followed with a rubber roller, making sure no edges curled up. After waiting thirty minutes, they rolled up the other part and repeated the process. By the time they were finished, it was nine o'clock and probably a hundred degrees in the shade.

"Let's take a break before we bring the furniture back up," Jennifer said.

Downstairs, they sipped cold drinks and fanned themselves.

"Are you up for a hike?" Mogi asked.

"A hike? I figured we'd do another dive. Why do you want to go on a hike?"

"Well, I've been thinking."

"Uh-oh. That's always a bad sign."

"No, come on, really. I've been thinking about the professor's mysterious mark."

"I thought you decided that he was toast."

Mogi smiled. "Well, yeah, but maybe he's left out something."

"Okay, out with it. What have you been thinking?"

"Suppose I was Butch Cassidy and I had outlaw friends, like Harvey Logan, who had not been along the trail going through White Canyon. I would put a mark on the canyon entrance so he could find his way to the trail, right?"

"Right."

"So, what happens when Harvey comes back? Now he wants to take the White Canyon trail to get *into* the Colorado River basin. Coming out of a canyon is no guarantee that you'll recognize it going the other direction, so I think he'd need some kind of mark to help him."

"Well," Jennifer said slowly, "I don't know what it looks like, but the canyon entrance might be obvious when you come from the Colorado direction."

"Yeah, maybe. But if I haven't been in that country before, I would still want some mark that guaranteed that I wasn't going down the wrong canyon."

"Okay. That seems reasonable. So what?"

"Well, okay then, suppose Butch did put a mark at the east entrance of White Canyon. I bet it would be the same mark that he used on the west entrance."

"You still haven't solved the problem. You still don't know what Butch's mark looked like."

"Right. But if the professor were to take pictures of all the marks at the east end of the canyon and compare them to those pictures he's taken of the west end, I bet that if a mark at one end matched a mark at the other end, they would have been put there by the same person. And if that mark didn't show up any place else around this country, they would definitely have been created to mark the canyon's entrances."

Jennifer crossed her arms, rolled her eyes toward the ceiling, and then said, "You want to hike to the east entrance, don't you?"

"Well, hey, that's a great idea! I'd be happy to go along! According to the map, we can motor up the canyon to where the water ends and take a trail that goes several miles to the east. If we see any marks on the walls, we'll photograph them to compare to the professor's to find any matches."

"That might actually be interesting, dork-boy," Jennifer said. "I wonder what we would find. Should we tell Dr. Hawthorne about it before we go, or wait until we actually find some marks or something?"

"Let's wait. He was going to make a dive this morning and then park the sub and let the batteries charge up. Remember when I thought the boat was sinking? He's got a winch attached to the ceiling of the cabin. When he's moving the houseboat or when he's recharging the batteries, he hooks it onto the sub and lifts it out of the water. That makes the houseboat hold the weight of the sub, so it sits lower in the water. When he winches the sub down so that it floats, the houseboat sits higher in the water. Ta-da! Mystery solved."

"Huh. Okay, well, if we go on this hike, we need to be back in time for a shower. I'd like to clean up before the fireworks show. By the way, Dr. Hawthorne seemed really happy when I invited him to go with us to the fireworks. I think he gets lonely out here."

Mogi looked at his watch and counted the hours backward. "The fireworks show starts at nine o'clock tonight. It will take us more than an hour to motor down to Bullfrog, plus we'll need to eat at the marina beforehand. Eight, seven, six. Throwing in time to get gas, that means we need to leave here by about five-thirty."

"What time did the professor tell us to pick him up at his place?"

"Four o'clock. He's hoping to have any pictures from this morning's dive printed out and ready to show us. If we're also going to have pictures to show him, we'd better get a move on."

———

It was a long hike. They made it far enough that the land around them was no longer bordered by cliffs.

Working their way back, Mogi took several pictures of anything that might qualify as a mark, including several handprints, spirals, sun symbols, snakes, and a couple of figures. All but one of them appeared several times. The one that was not repeated was a different-looking hand symbol: Instead of the hand being splayed out, showing all the fingers distinctly, this hand was closed, the fingers and thumb together, the whole figure straight up and down, like the position of the hand in a salute.

It had been pecked out of the dark varnish on the side of a sandstone wall and was probably twice the size of a real hand.

Hiking several miles through the ups and downs of slickrock country, with the sunlight radiating off the hard surfaces around them, Mogi and Jennifer were hot and glad to get back to the little speedboat. They were soon loving being drenched by the spray of water coming over the prow. As they rounded the last curve of the upper bay, Mogi suddenly throttled back and the boat's prow sank quickly into the water. Jennifer and Mogi stared in surprise.

The professor's houseboat was gone.

Mogi pushed the throttle up and cut a wide circle around the bay. There was no sign of the houseboat. The McDowells' houseboat was as they'd left it, and the new one that had come in the day before was anchored in the last curve in the upper part of the bay. All looked normal except that the strange-looking houseboat covered in solar panels was nowhere to be seen.

"What's going on?" Jennifer asked.

"I have no idea," Mogi replied. "He knew we were coming, and he's the one who set the time. He didn't seem overly absentminded to me, so something must have happened. Maybe he found something underwater that made him move it to a different location."

Mogi swung the boat in a quick arc and made for the bay's entrance. Out in the lake, he motored up and down while he and Jennifer looked along the shore for any evidence of the old houseboat. They even made a short tour of Farley Canyon Bay.

There was nothing. The professor was gone.

Mogi turned the speedboat and headed back to the houseboat. After tying the boat to the stern, they discussed the professor's absence over cold drinks.

"Maybe something went wrong with the panels and he needed a part. He probably went up to the marina," Jennifer said.

"That doesn't make sense. He would have taken his fishing boat."

"Maybe something needed a fix that required a mechanic."

"He's an engineer. I can't imagine that he hasn't fixed everything on that boat at least twice already. Besides, he wouldn't let anybody even close to getting inside for fear of being discovered."

"Maybe he found something and needed someone else to look at it?"

"Maybe, but it doesn't seem likely."

They finally decided that whatever Hawthorne

had done, it had required a hasty departure that hadn't left him enough time to write a note.

———

Following their schedule, they left the houseboat at about five o'clock. Mogi pushed the throttle slowly and cut a large curve across the bay, still trying to figure out what events could have caused the professor to leave. He absolutely hated unanswered questions.

His arc was big enough that it brought them close to the new houseboat up the bay. Mogi glanced at the big rig and then suddenly cut back the engine.

"Look," he called out to Jennifer. Pulled up behind the big houseboat was the professor's fishing boat. Its engine was barely sticking out from behind the large pontoons.

Mogi motored up close. "Do you see anything wrong?" he asked Jennifer, who was leaning over the side and giving the boat a good look.

"Not a thing," she said. "It's certainly the professor's, but I don't see any reason that it would be tied up over here."

"And hidden," Mogi replied. "Like somebody didn't want it to be found." He shook his head. "At least we know the houseboat didn't sink—his little boat would have gone down with it. Maybe something went wrong, Hawthorne needed help right away, and this guy got involved. They needed the newer speedboat, so he tied his boat here and they both took off with the houseboat pulling the new speedboat."

"But," Jennifer replied, "if it had been an emergency, they would have left the houseboat and gone in the speedboat. Or they would have taken this houseboat. It's got to be at least twice as fast as the professor's. Even the McDowells' houseboat would be faster, and it's a real clunker."

"So it must not have been an emergency. What else could it have been?"

Once again, there was no easy explanation.

———

The Fourth of July celebration was a big deal at the lake.

Bullfrog Marina and its surrounding lake area were crowded with an armada of houseboats, speedboats, sailboats, and jet skis. A roped-off area allowed hundreds of people to float in the water while music blasted from different sound systems. An official marina bandstand had bands playing throughout the afternoon, drawing a raucous crowd in inner tubes, floating trampolines, and inflated loungers, with plenty of buoyant beer coolers.

People were everywhere. The fireworks were to be launched from the cliffs across from the marina, leaving the large bay next to it to be filled with even more boats.

Mogi picked his way through the various vessels to get close to the fueling dock. There seemed to be some order to who was in line and who wasn't, so he patiently waited as others pulled up to the dock attendants ferrying long hoses out to the boats.

While idly watching the activity and admiring some of the fancier crafts, Mogi glanced ahead to the front of the fueling dock as a huge houseboat was pulling away. Hidden behind it, already next to the dock, was an old houseboat covered in solar panels.

The professor's.

The teens watched as a slender man talked with the attendant who filled the gas tanks on the houseboat and the speedboat tied in the back. It might have been the same man who had come into the bay the afternoon before, but it was hard to see clearly.

Mogi tried to nudge closer to the dock, but the boats were packed in around him. "We'll catch up with him," he said. "He'll be ahead by a few minutes, but we can easily catch up."

Jennifer looked skeptical. "We ought to leave him alone, you know. If the professor wants to pick up and move, it's his business. Just because we don't know the reason doesn't mean he doesn't have one. We don't need to be barging in on his private business."

"But there's something wrong."

"Maybe, maybe not. We don't know anything for sure. In fact, nothing really even looks wrong, does it? Maybe he met the guy this afternoon and had a new idea of something to do. We weren't there, so he figured he'd just go on without us."

They debated back and forth, and Mogi finally decided she was right.

After the fireworks show, it was a long, dark ride back to White Canyon, slowed sometimes to a crawl by the boat traffic. Though the boating lanes were lit by lights on the buoys, keeping correct distances and anticipating the movements of other boats kept both of them busy.

Mogi kept thinking about the little houseboat.

He hated unanswered questions.

CHAPTER 14

It was his best day ever. Dr. Death couldn't believe his luck, especially since the day before had been his worst day ever.

After anchoring his houseboat in White Canyon Bay the previous afternoon, the man had taken his speedboat up to the bridge to work out the details for setting the explosives.

The first bad news was that there wasn't much backed-up water beneath the bridge. The lake was at the lowest level of its history, caused by years of drought in most of the western United States. Lack of rain, lack of snowfall, and shrinking run-off from rivers all contributed to the lake's low water level.

The shallow water meant that to keep the explosives hidden in the water, he would have to place them farther away from the side of the canyon that held the bridge's concrete pier. Noting the distance, he knew that the explosion wouldn't cause enough damage to open up the hole in the cliff beneath the pier.

The second bit of bad news was that the water was murky. He couldn't even see his hand when he stuck it in the water over the side of the boat. He'd have to connect the explosives before he put them in the water, which would make it impossible to connect all the boxes.

It was not possible to do what he had come to do.

Dr. Death rammed the throttle of the boat to its max and drove like a madman, yelling, screaming, hammering the dash, tearing across the surface of the water.

His destiny had been denied him again! He was back to nothing. Not only could he not blow up the dam, he couldn't even blow up a lousy bridge!

Back at the houseboat, kicking and scattering his books and papers across the floor as he stomped through, he grabbed two cans of beer and stalked up the stairs to the upper deck. He slammed himself into a deck chair, drained the first can in one swig, and was halfway through the next one before he calmed down.

Fifteen minutes later, his violent anger had given way to depression and sorrow. It just wasn't fair. He had held the vision for so long and had worked so hard, yet he was being prevented from being who he was meant to be.

America was supposed to be the place where people could make their dreams come true, but his dream was being denied at every turn.

He sat in the chair for hours, wallowing in self-pity and bemoaning his bad luck, staring hopelessly across the bay.

By the next morning, Dr. Death's bad mood had drifted away. He had been defeated at every turn but had convinced himself that it was all for the best. He had to be patient. Even if all his plans were scrapped, the explosives could be used for something else in the future. And he was still far, far away from that little cell. He could enjoy the houseboat if nothing else, and maybe even go for a dive in the clear waters.

Nothing of consequence would happen this Fourth of July—no explosives, no deaths, no bridge falling into the river. No one knew what was supposed to have happened, so no one knew that it didn't happen. It was a good thing he hadn't created a stir of publicity about it.

It just wasn't his time, he decided.

He was sitting in the same chair as the evening before—watching the whole lot of nothing around him, idly taking in the heat of the morning, the bare rocks, the motionless water—when he saw it happen.

The old houseboat across the bay rose up in the water.

If he had glanced away for a moment, he would never have seen it. But staring gave him enough of a mental delay to notice the difference in how deep the pontoons on the old houseboat sat in the water before they suddenly and mysteriously rose out of the water by at least a foot.

What in the world?

As he watched, now through his binoculars, the water around the boat gave a sudden churn, and then all was still.

The man grew curious. He knew that he had not imagined it, but there was no earthly reason for it to happen. After watching for several more minutes, he got up, changed into his swimsuit, retrieved his dive equipment, geared up, stepped down the ladder into the water, and was just submerging as the speedboat with the good-looking girl and her boyfriend zipped by.

He kept himself hidden from them and then disappeared below the surface.

The man had learned to dive off the coast of California.

It came naturally, and he loved being alone in a world so completely different from the one he lived in above the water. He joined the Navy, volunteering for Dive School.

He had done all right, but the officers were jerks. He made it into underwater demolition work but was scuttled out of the program when it looked like he enjoyed the destruction too much. They said they couldn't trust him.

Okay, well, he really did like blowing things up, but wasn't that the point? He didn't understand what the problem was.

Once drummed out of the program, he kept up his skills with recreational diving, mainly on World War II wrecks off the coast of Hawaii. It was what he missed most after he landed in prison—the freedom of the ocean and the complete isolation that it brought.

Dr. Death tested out his respirator, slipped down to ten feet, and leveled out. The water felt good. Very good. The swim was several hundred yards, but he was barely warmed up when he slipped under the old houseboat and worked his way around the opening between the pontoons.

Cautiously, he surfaced inside.

At first, he thought somebody had built a platform for raising sunken boats. Then he thought maybe it was for raising and lowering a diving bell or some other sort of research vessel that lowered people into deep water. It was only after taking a couple of turns around the floor opening that he finally decided it had to be some sort of diving machine, maybe even a mini-sub. Too many battery connections, too many pictures of underwater sites, too many tools.

Not to mention the winch attached to the ceiling.

It had to be used for lowering and raising something, which was probably what caused the houseboat to rise in the water. Something had been winched up, then was winched down, and was now elsewhere.

The more he thought about it, the more it *had* to be a submarine.

The clouds parted, the sun shone down, and Dr. Death realized that all was now possible. All the failures along the way must have been meant to lead him to this moment.

Dr. Death was back in business.

He slipped beneath the water and swam to the

small fishing boat tied to the back railing. Floating gently next to the motor, he knew he couldn't be seen in the watery shadows. He turned off his air tank and hung in the darkness, waiting.

A half-hour later, he felt a vibration in the water. Using his goggles, he watched as an odd-looking mini-sub made a slow curve to line up under the open rectangle, stopped, gently rose, and then fit precisely into the hollowed floor of the houseboat.

Dr. Death turned his air back on, swam forward, and hovered off to the side of the opening between the pontoons to watch the sub being winched up into its berth.

Amazed, excited, and vastly curious, he focused on the difference having a small submarine was going to make for him. All the planning he had done for months would not be wasted. All the media coverage and all the fame would once again be his. His dream would come true!

He was going to blow up that lovely, lovely dam!

Dr. Death quietly removed his dive harness, buckled it onto the superstructure beneath the houseboat, and watched until the sub pilot had hooked up the batteries and gone into a different room. Quietly, he lifted himself from the water onto the walkway, rubbed himself off to remove the sound of dripping water, and then confronted the surprised pilot. The old geezer was quickly bound and gagged.

The man whose destiny had repeatedly been stolen from him was now a new man, almost giddy, dancing up and down the walkway. He looked the sub over carefully, immediately recognizing how it functioned. He reviewed the gauges, valves, and levers and then looked over the hardware that serviced the sub within the equipment bay.

Using straps alongside the walkway, he secured the submarine in its cradle, retrieved his diving gear, pulled up the two anchors, started the motor, and moved the old houseboat across the bay. Heading in carefully, he swung it alongside his larger houseboat.

He moved the boxes of explosives from his houseboat to the older one, stacking them beneath the solar panels on the roof. The man checked and rechecked his maps and books and took only what was critical. The dive equipment, ropes, and food went into his own speedboat, which he would pull behind the old houseboat.

He'd use the sub to place the explosives along the right side of the dam, next to the cliff. Once the timer was set, he'd anchor the old junker in a cove someplace and then race up the lake as fast as the speedboat could go. He'd set the timer for several hours, long enough to give himself a good margin to work with. Once the dam was broken, the lake would drain like a bathtub, and he wanted to get the houseboat back to the marina, unload his stuff, and be out of the area before it all happened.

Dr. Death shoved the old fishing boat behind the pontoons of his own houseboat, tied his speedboat behind the old houseboat, and then chugged down the bay. It would be a long, slow trip to the dam, but a renewed spirit made him feel alive and vital, like he was a member of a very important family on a very important mission.

Dr. Death, Outlaw, was ready.

In his head, he revived the dreams of a major action, of causing vast destruction with a single sweep of his hand.

He would glory in being a Great One. He might be a day late getting it done, but the Fourth of July weekend would still be remembered as the day Glen Canyon Dam crumbled under the roar of the mighty Colorado, and a nation was devastated.

He could hardly wait.

CHAPTER 15

It was bad enough he'd been up at six o'clock the previous morning, but Mogi now stood next to the upper deck railing at five o'clock, the sky showing only a glow from the sunrise in the east.

He was staring at the empty spot of water across the bay where the professor's houseboat had sat the morning before, ticking off a list in his head:

1. The professor was gone, his houseboat was gone, and the sub was gone.

2. The professor had missed going to the fireworks with Mogi and Jennifer.

3. The small fishing boat had been secreted behind the large houseboat farther up the bay.

4. The man from the large houseboat was probably the same man who was driving the professor's houseboat, the one who filled up the gas tanks the night before.

5. The man driving the professor's houseboat headed down the lake, not up, so he was not returning to where the smaller houseboat had been anchored, which meant that the sub was no longer going to be used to make dives on the professor's site.

The more items he listed in his mind, the more questions he had:

6. Why would the professor leave his dive site when he wasn't finished searching for Butch Cassidy's mark?

7. Why didn't the professor leave a note telling them he wouldn't be going to the fireworks show?

8. Why would the man be driving the small houseboat instead of the professor?

9. If they were making a trip down the lake, why wouldn't they take the faster houseboat?

10. Why pull the newer speedboat with the smaller houseboat when it would put a big load on the engines?

11. Why was the small fishing boat hidden?

12. The large houseboat seemed to be unoccupied. Why would the man rent it and then leave it unattended?

"You hate getting up early. What in the world are you doing?" Jennifer asked as she came up behind him. She hadn't slept well either.

He looked at her, his eyes weary. He was hungry and his body was tired, but his mind was bouncing all over the place. "I just hate things that I can't figure out."

Jennifer looked at the empty spot across the bay.

"Maybe they just went for a tourist cruise."

Mogi knew she didn't believe that was a real possibility.

"We need to do something," he said.

"Like what?"

"Like go over and have a look inside that big houseboat." He pointed up the bay.

"Wouldn't that be breaking and entering?"

"Well... I wasn't going to break anything. I bet there's a window open or something."

"That's still trespassing. Your mother taught you better."

"Well, yeah, but she also taught me to help out people caught in bad situations if I can."

"You don't know that this is a bad situation."

He looked at her with a questioning face.

"Yeah, well, okay... It looks like a bad situation," she said. "But it doesn't mean that we should necessarily go poking around somebody else's houseboat."

"I'll tell you what," Mogi said. "How about if we just casually motor up next to that houseboat and look in the windows. If there's somebody there, which there isn't because the speedboat is gone, then we'll just say that the waves caught us and forced us too close to it."

"And we'd be casually motoring by at five in the morning?"

Mogi shook his head. "Trust me—we won't find anyone. And maybe we'll find something that will tell us if the professor is in trouble or not. Then, if he's not, we can at least stop worrying."

Jennifer looked across at the big houseboat, then

over to the empty spot where the professor's house-boat had been, and then back again. "Okay. But we do it as quietly as we can, and if we see someone inside, we apologize and leave, okay?"

It took about ten minutes to get the speedboat started, unhitched, up the bay, and innocently floating next to the large houseboat. Jennifer made all sorts of shushing motions to get Mogi to be more cautious and to look in the windows first, but he was immediately over the railing.

He'd been gone for only a minute when she saw the front door open and her brother walk out.

"Whoever it is isn't too smart. He locked the door right next to an open window."

"Let's not tell Mom and Dad this part, okay?" she said.

With the sun not yet over the canyon rim, it was dark inside. They passed through the main cabin and checked the bedrooms first, just to make sure no one was home, and then turned on the lights.

"Good grief! Come look at this," Jennifer called to Mogi from the back bedroom. She was standing next to a bed stacked with comic books. There must have been two hundred of them.

"Wow," Mogi said, glancing at some of the covers.

"Some of these are classics. Who would bring them on a houseboat?"

The next bedroom was mostly bare but tidy. The bed sheets and light blanket were smooth and tight, and the clothes hung up and neatly folded. Two luggage bags sat in the corner. The bathroom had been used, but barely.

The third bedroom had stacks of medium-sized ice chests, ten in all. Each of them was empty.

Mogi was bewildered. "What in the world?"

The living and dining rooms were also interesting.

A large, marked-up map of the Glen Canyon Recreation Area was spread across the sofa, along with photos of Hite Marina, the north end of the lake, Glen Canyon Dam, and the south end of the lake. A small stack of books and papers sat on an end table.

Unfolded across the dining room table was an enlargement of a map of the dam area. It showed the dam, the road above, the tourist facility next to the dam site, and the bays in and around the area. Small lines were drawn at angles in front of the dam, with groups of numbers scribbled in various places.

Several small marks made a curve along the west side of the dam, on the lake side, right where the dam joined the cliff.

Mogi was puzzling over the map when he heard Jennifer say, "Uh-oh."

She was looking at the three books on the end table: Naval Undersea Explosives, Controller Design for Demolition Work, and Impact Management for Dispersed Charges.

Mogi whistled softly. "What's going on here?"

"I don't know," Jennifer said, "but it looks like someone is planning on blowing up something."

———

The speedboat spurted over the waves of the lake.

"Did we get everything?" Mogi called over his shoulder. They had hurried back to the McDowells' houseboat, leaving the big houseboat untouched.

"I got all the dive equipment and this unopened box of donuts. Have at it."

Mogi grabbed what he could, stuffed them into his mouth, and hung on.

What a time to have no cell service! Now they had to do everything the hard way. Hite Marina was the closest place they thought a park ranger would be. It was still early in the morning, and the boat traffic was mostly fishermen leaving the docks and launch ramps to make it to the shallow water of the coves.

Mogi throttled back as soon as they got into the marina area and headed for the main dock. He wasn't sure what to do, so he picked an empty spot and pulled in. "You'd better stay here in case somebody wants to chase us off," he said. "I'll find a ranger."

Jennifer nodded, sat back on the bench seat, and thought about what they had found.

The maps spread across the sofa and table showed details for the south end of the lake, especially of the dam area.

If someone was going to blow up the dam, why rent a houseboat a hundred-plus miles away? Why have detailed maps of the north end? And what did the professor have to do with it? She shook her head. She didn't believe that he had anything to do with it, so it had to be his submarine. What if someone knew he had it and was stealing it? But how could they have known about it? Had they killed Hawthorne and stolen his houseboat?

The books were about handling underwater explosives.

That was pretty scary, but the professor's houseboat was full of books about outlaws and bandits. Maybe the guy was just a friendly Navy SEAL on vacation. Had they read too much into it? Who would be crazy enough to blow up the dam at Lake Powell, anyway?

She thought of the protestors at the visitor center. They certainly wanted the dam gone, but would anyone actually do it? Was this them?

And what's the deal with the comic books? Did she and her brother just invade some family's vacation? Are they getting themselves into a lot of trouble? Were they being really stupid?

"You still with us?" Mogi asked as he jumped into the boat.

"Oh, yeah, just a little foggy. I never got my coffee. Did you find a ranger?"

"Nope. Everybody in law enforcement was out all night chasing illegal fireworks and drunks. I had to leave a note about what we found."

"So, now what?" Jennifer asked as Mogi was backing the boat out and turning around.

Mogi's face became grim. "I figure that the guy we saw last night with the professor's houseboat is taking the sub to the dam where he's going to use it to plant explosives, just like the marks indicated on the map. It's not a given that the park rangers are going to believe us, so it's up to us to stop him. If nothing else, we've got to help the professor."

"I was afraid you'd say something like that," Jennifer said.

Past the marina boundary, Mogi hit the throttle and the speedboat jumped forward, slicing through the water and throwing up a spray of water that made both of them cold.

———

"Mornin', Ray."

"Hey, Bobby, how's business this morning?"

"Ah, too many people with hangovers to want anything. My beer sold out yesterday, and I don't have any hot dogs left, so I expect I'm stuck with selling fishing worms for the day. Hardly worth opening up. I've only had one guy in here this morning, and he was looking for you. He's discovered a terrorist plot to blow up the dam."

"Is that right?"

"Sure thing. A kid came in about forty-five minutes ago with a wild tale about finding a houseboat up White Canyon that had all sorts of maps and drawings and had a bunch of books about explosives and underwater demolition and stuff. He left you a note."

The ranger read Mogi's note and laughed.

"We get a hundred threats a year from someone who's out to blow up the dam. I haven't been down south today, but I'm willing to bet the dam is still there. This kid just ran across somebody who was serious about their fireworks display or video game. We get them all the time."

"Yeah, but your usual threats are from amateurs. This terrorist is an authentic bad boy, no doubt about it. You want to know how I know? It's because he has business cards. I mean, he must be a professional to have business cards, right?" He chuckled. "Check this out."

The boat-dock concession manager handed over a card. "The kid found a bunch of them spread around the houseboat."

The ranger held it up in the light. On one side was printed: *DR. DEATH, OUTLAW.*

On the opposite side was written: *THE FOURTH OF JULY.*

This time, he really laughed.

"I'm going to have to call this one in. You know ol' Alice at headquarters, down in Page? Alice Humbredt? She's a good egg. Anyway, she collects stories about the loonies we get around here. She'll really like this one."

CHAPTER 16

D r. Death cursed the slow, lumbering beast of a houseboat. The single outboard motor in the rear was big but old and hardly put out more than a wheezy chug-chug to get the heavily laden vessel down the lake. He was hoping it wouldn't give out. That would ruin everything.

After filling up at Bullfrog Marina the evening before, he had driven half the night, finally pulling over into a small canyon to sleep for a few hours. The geezer had moaned and shuffled until more sleeping pills were stuffed in his mouth, and then all was quiet.

As the morning sun was peeking over the cliffs, the man pulled up the anchor and resumed the journey. He stopped for gas at Dangling Rope Marina and then kept on down the lake until they left the narrow canyons and entered the expansive waters of lower Lake Powell.

And then, there it was.

The dam was bigger than it looked from the highway.

The man turned the motor off and drifted next to the cliffs on the right side, outside of the chained-off area.

Using binoculars, he examined each side of the dam, looking at where the huge, concrete structure fit into the cliffs of the canyon wall. Nothing short of an atomic bomb could break the massive dam, but a lot less was needed if nature could help. His plan was to smash the rock as close to the dam as possible and let the pressure squeeze water into the cracks.

It wouldn't take much. Even a small leak would act like a high-pressure hose, scouring increasingly larger holes, and the increasing volume of water would be like a cutting blade. Bigger leaks would bring vibrations that would act like jackhammers, pounding both the concrete and the rock and battering the structures until chunks of concrete and rock were broken away. Water would plow through the openings as if through a fire hydrant, and the side of the dam would collapse completely.

The man had goose pimples imagining it. The destruction would be his victory, his defining moment, a ceremony for his induction into the family of the Great Ones.

All he had to do was ferry the explosives underwater to the dam, place them in a line going up the face of the rock next to the dam, connect them, set the timer, and escape up the lake in the speedboat.

Dr. Death pulled the houseboat into a narrow bay

about a half-mile from the dam, tucked it behind an outcropping of sandstone, and dropped anchor.

———

Jennifer's hands were shaking, her whole body was sore.

Handling a speedboat on and off for six hours was taking a toll on her muscles and nerves. She and Mogi traded off driving the boat down the lake, stopping to refuel at Bullfrog and then at Dangling Rope, but otherwise, they had kept the accelerator handle pushed to the max.

Even sitting in the passenger seat, Mogi felt battered, the boat constantly slamming up and down against the lake's waves. The McDowells' speedboat was no race winner, but it had done well, moving quickly in and out of the narrow waterways, the engine consistently powering the craft as fast as it could go.

When the dam appeared in the distance, Mogi moved up to the windshield and stood next to Jennifer. Someplace ahead was Hawthorne's houseboat. He was hoping the professor was alive and the bad man was gone. Even if they couldn't prevent the dam from being bombed, they had to get to the professor.

How much time was needed to set up this sort of thing? Where would he put the explosives? How much would it take? How many trips with the sub to plant the explosives? Would the sub batteries stay charged long enough? What kind of detonator—a timer? Radio-controlled? Do remote controls even work underwater? How big would the explosion be? Could you actually blow up all that concrete?

Would the man do it immediately? Would he wait until morning? Has he learned to drive the sub? Would he kill the professor if he didn't need him anymore?

Who was this guy, anyway?

It was another hot day on Lake Powell, but Mogi's sweat was not from the temperature.

———

They couldn't find it.

The Franklins motored up and down the vicinity of the dam, went back and forth across the canyons and around Wahweap Marina, circled the big buttresses of stone that stood hundreds of feet above the surface of the lake, and drove through every cove they could see.

There was no sign of Hawthorne's houseboat.

"I bet we haven't hit half of the possible places you could hide a houseboat," Mogi said as he flopped down in the passenger seat.

"Well, we can't do much more today," Jennifer said.

"We're about to lose the daylight, so we won't be able to see anything anyway. How about we make it to the marina, check in with the rangers, and then get something to eat. I'm starving! And where are we going to stay tonight?"

"Uh, well, I don't know, but I'm with you on the food idea."

Mogi took over the wheel.

————

It was a stunningly beautiful morning on one of the premier freshwater lakes in the world, but Dr. Death didn't notice.

He was up early, playing inside the sub. He had held off on the sedatives so the geezer could answer some questions. He'd refused at first, but the man beat him, convincing him that he might as well talk.

Eventually, Dr. Death figured out how the sub operated. Pretty simple, he thought. The old guy had made everything automatic. Push the stick forward to sink, pull back to rise, and push to either side to turn. No foot pedals like an airplane. The manipulating arms outside were controlled by pulling, pushing, or turning handles. A simple throttle controlled the propellers, to go forward or backward.

I can do this, he thought.

"You can't do it, you know," the geezer said through his swollen lips. "It took me years to design and build this, and then a hundred hours to learn how to drive it right."

"Shut up, old man. You don't know me. You don't know what I can do."

"I know you're an idiot. Whatever you're planning to do, it's not going to happen."

"You haven't figured out what I'm doing?"

The geezer was silent.

Dr. Death laughed. "Well, I tell you what, old man. Because I'm a nice guy, and you're an old fool who happened to be in the wrong place at the wrong time, I'll tell you what I'm going to do, and then I'll give you a choice.

"First, I'm going to plant quite a lot of explosives up real close to the right side of the dam, snugged right against the rock. Second, I'm going to light them up. The shock wave will fracture the rock, hopefully up and down the seam, so that lots of water will find its way between the rock and the cement. The water pressure will cause the dam to break, and all the water in this beautiful lake will rush down to the Gulf of Mexico, killing hundreds of thousands of people and disrupting life in America for years to come."

The geezer closed his eyes.

"All due to my wonderful luck of discovering your submarine. It wasn't going to happen, you see, because I couldn't get the explosives close enough to the dam on my own. But, here we are—about to snatch victory from the jaws of defeat!"

Dr. Death laughed again.

"Okay, now, about the choice. Here it is: I'll tie you up outside and you can watch the beginning of the destruction of the entire western United States. You can struggle as you and your crummy houseboat get caught up in the currents and finally get sucked into the break like soap scum in a bathtub drain."

The geezer shuddered and opened his eyes.

"Or, I'll give you a little more sleepy-time medicine, and you can drown in your sleep. You think about it while I'm practicing with my new ride."

"Why are you doing this?" the geezer asked, his cracked lips bleeding. "Even radical environmentalists aren't dumb enough to let all the water out at one time. Are you a California-hater? Are you insane? Did your mommy abandon you when you were a baby? Or are you just a pathetic loser out to make a big name for himself?"

The younger man gave the geezer a stern look.

"There's not a thing wrong with me, you overeducated jerk. I'm doing this because I want to do it. I want to do it so that people will know who I am and what I can do. It is my destiny. It's not something you'd understand.

"And, by the way, you just lost your choice. I'm going to make sure you watch until the water swirls down your throat."

Dr. Death closed the cockpit window, secured it with the inside latches, and bobbed in the houseboat opening for a minute. He flipped the clearly marked switches for powering the water and air pumps, turned on the lights, and made sure the power to the propellers was on.

He pushed the control stick forward, and the sub slowly sank beneath the water.

CHAPTER 17

"There! Over there!"

Jennifer jumped to Mogi's side as she followed his pointing finger.

Barely peeking out from behind a canyon wall, the professor's houseboat had drifted exactly right to reflect the early morning sun of the panels.

It had been a long night. The teens had made it to the Wahweap Marina, filled up their gas tank, and then hurried to the park headquarters, but the office was closed.

The main dispatch office for the park rangers was located in Page, a few miles away, so the office wasn't required to be staffed during the night.

After searching the marina—it had closed early after the holiday—for any other kind of official, they wrote another note. They explained who they were and what was happening, described their boat and the professor's houseboat, and slid the note under the door to the office.

Using as much change as they could gather between them, they bought snacks and drinks from the machines outside the bait shop and then laid out cushions in the boat for their beds. Quickly learning that the idea of being rocked to sleep by gentle waves was an outright lie, they struggled through a miserable night.

After accepting that they would not sleep, they left the marina after sunrise. An hour later, they discovered the houseboat's hiding place.

"Now what do we do?" Jennifer asked as Mogi turned the boat and passed by the entrance to the alcove.

"We can't be seen, first of all," Mogi replied. "If the professor is on the houseboat, we need to get him off. But we need to know if the bad guy is on the houseboat before we try anything. I'll swim over to see if the sub is there. If it's not, I'll get inside and see if the professor is still there. If he's there, we'll get him into our boat and find out if the guy has already planted the explosives."

"What if the sub is there?"

Mogi thought for a moment. "I don't think the sub can carry all the explosives in one trip. The guy will have to make several trips, and the smart thing would be to move the houseboat closer to the dam to make each trip as short as possible. So, if we can't get the professor now, we can get him after the houseboat is moved and the sub has left."

Mogi sorted out the scuba gear from under the

back seat and had his tank and its harness on in a few minutes.

Jennifer grabbed her brother's arm and looked into his eyes. "If you see something stupid to do, don't do it, all right?"

He smiled. "You betcha. I promise. Safety first."

Jennifer made sure he had his emergency inflation vest on and then helped him fall backward over the side of the boat.

———

Dr. Death carefully floated the sub back into its berth, raised the cockpit window, and froze.

The geezer was gone.

He heard nothing. He slowly climbed out of the sub and moved quietly to the front bedroom. From his bag on the floor, he retrieved a pistol, checked the chamber, and then moved back through the cabin.

A lot of water had been dripped on the walkway, right where the geezer had been tied. That meant someone had come through the sub opening.

The man followed the wet spots outside. There was water on the deck next to the railing as well. Clearly, someone had come through the opening, untied the geezer, and loaded him into a boat. He carefully searched the rest of the houseboat but found no one.

Dr. Death, Outlaw, lost it.

Shaking, yelling, sweating, crying, stomping up and down the walkways, he raged against his situation. He had been revealed! Discovered! Ratted out? Not possible.

Who could have known? Everything had happened at the last minute. It wasn't possible that someone found out.

Who could have...

That girl and her boyfriend! They were the only ones in the bay, the only ones who had been close to the old man's houseboat. Maybe they were cops! Maybe they'd been watching him the whole time!

The loneliest man on Earth went through as many scenarios as he could, but none of them kept him from the panic, the frantic realization of being discovered, the utter frustration of having all his work ruined.

Breathe. Relax. Focus. Breathe. Relax. Focus. Breathe. Relax. Focus.

Slowly, finally, the man calmed down.

It was over. If he were arrested now, it would be for kidnapping. Having the explosives and the guns would brand him a terrorist. He'd beat up the old guy pretty good, so that's assault. And he'd stolen the houseboat. And the fake license and credit card...

Eight steps up, eight steps back. For a long, long time.

He couldn't do it. He wouldn't do it.

He had to run.

Okay, he was going to run, but what about the houseboat and the explosives? Man, he hated to lose those explosives! They were expensive, and his supplier might be angry if they ended up in the cops' hands. Maybe he should go ahead and blow every-thing up. As a matter of fact, he could use the explosives to create a diversion for his escape—that was good.

Could he still blow up the dam?

He didn't think so. He only had minutes. Whoever had taken the geezer might already be talking to the park rangers, so using the sub to plant the explosives was out.

Wait...back in White Canyon Bay, he had loaded the explosives on top of the old man's houseboat, so the boxes were together. He only needed to connect each box and set a timer. That would give him a good-sized explosion.

Suppose he set the houseboat next to the restricted area chain? In fact, if he sank the houseboat with all the boxes wired together, the whole mess might fall alongside the cliff. The blast would be too far from the dam to do any good, but if the explosives detonated right alongside the cliff, it might fracture the rock enough to cause a rockslide, which might cause the cliff to give way, which might weaken the seam next to the dam.

The more he thought about it, the more reasonable it became. Why not?

He might still get headlines out of this.

———

Alice Humbredt didn't work on Sundays, so it wasn't until Monday morning that she got the voicemail from Ray about the business card. She was still chuckling when she noticed the piece of paper on the floor in front of the door. Anything shoved through the mail slot was usually a complaint from a fisherman angry that the do-it-yourself gas pumps weren't working or from somebody reporting loud behavior at a campground.

What Alice did not usually receive was a handwritten note about kidnapped professors, explosives, and submarines.

She was considering what to do when the radio squawked.

It was Ray. He had gone to White Canyon Bay that morning. Remembering the note from the day before, he had located the houseboat and done a search. As soon as he'd entered the cabin, he knew the threat was real.

He'd been in Iraq, and he knew the smell of the packaging that explosives came in.

That got Alice out of her chair.

"Ray!" she screamed. "My God, Ray! Somebody's going to blow the dam!"

She told him of the message on the paper.

"Alice. ALICE!" Ray spoke over the radio. "Get your response list out and follow it. We need Homeland Security to be contacted, and the FBI, the State Police, and the dispatch desk. You have all those numbers on your response list. I'm going to radio everybody that I can reach and send them your way."

"MYGODRAYSOMEBODY'SGOINGTO-BLOWTHEDAM!"

"Alice. ALICE!" Ray repeated. "Do the checklist."

"THERE'SNOBODYHEREBUTMERAYWHAT-DOIDO?"

"Everybody's probably out in the canyons. Don't worry about them. I'll take care of them. You do your checklist. When you're done, get yourself armed and take out Boat 2, okay? Get on the lake and head to the dam, okay? You can do this, Alice. You'll know what to do when you get there."

Ray signed off.

Her hands shaking, she found the response paper and made the calls. Immediate threat. Immediate response needed. Threat verified. Threat confirmed. Attack underway.

Desperate to not talk to the phone anymore, Alice moved across the room, unlocked the arms cabinet, holstered a pistol, and loaded a short-barrel pump shotgun.

The phone was still ringing as she sprinted out the door and made for the ranger dock.

———

Hawthorne was a mess. His face was swollen, one eye socket was discolored, and he had bled heavily from his nose.

As soon as Mogi had gotten into the professor's houseboat and found him, he cut the plastic restraints on his wrists. It was awful: The zip ties had been pulled too tight, and the professor's hands were badly swollen, hanging useless from his wrists.

Mogi dragged him outside the houseboat and called to Jennifer. She motored over immediately. Once she was tied on, Mogi dropped his air tank and fins into the small boat and then struggled with his sister to get the professor on board.

Jennifer pushed the throttle to the max and headed for the marina. Mogi tried his best to cradle the professor's head to steady out the bumping and jarring of the boat.

Finally, struggling as he became more aware, the professor jerked against Mogi's arm. "He's going to blow the dam!" he shouted. "He's going to blow it up! We've got to—"

"We know!" Mogi shouted back over the roar of the motor. "We're going to catch him! Everything will be okay!"

"That idiot's going to use my sub! I didn't mean for it to be used like this! We've got to stop—"

"We're going to get him! Don't worry! We've got to get you to a doctor! Hang on, Dr. Hawthorne!"

Suddenly, the boat lurched as the motor was cut to nothing.

Mogi looked up to see Jennifer standing in the seat, frantically waving her arms. In the distance, a large speedboat raced toward them, with a massive canopy framework over the cockpit and flashing lights. As it turned and moved up next to them, he could see the twin outboard motors in the rear.

A ranger leaned over and secured a rope on the sidebars between the two boats.

"Are you Jennifer?" the ranger called out.

"Oh, yes, Officer, I am! We need some help!" Jennifer pointed to the professor, crumpled on the floor of the boat, his shirt soaked with blood.

Alice rummaged beneath a seat cushion for a first aid kit and jumped aboard the smaller boat. The ranger boat remained idling.

"Okay. Where's our bad guy right now?" Alice asked as she worked on the professor.

Mogi started giving her a detailed account of the morning.

"Just point. Where is he right now?"

They scanned the shoreline, looking for the alcove with the professor's houseboat, but were shocked to see that the houseboat moving across the lake, headed toward the dam.

Mogi knelt beside the professor. "Hawthorne! Did he have explosives? Where did he have the explosives?"

The professor struggled to answer. "On the roof. He put all the boxes on the roof."

Mogi jumped to the front seat and grabbed his binoculars. Focusing while the ranger continued to bandage the professor, Mogi could see the man bending over several boxes on the roof even as the houseboat continued to plow through the water. What was he doing? What about the sub?

He looked at Jennifer. "He knows he's been found out. He doesn't have time to do anything with the sub, so he's going straight for the dam."

He turned to the ranger, who had also noticed the houseboat moving.

"We've got to stop him!" Mogi shouted.

"*I've* got to stop him," Alice shouted back. "And *I* have to wait for backup. You need to get your friend back to the marina. I slowed the bleeding a little, but his nose is broken, and he's dehydrated. He needs to get to a doctor right away. That's what I want you two to do. I'll watch the bad guy until we can get some more rangers in on this."

Mogi looked at her with surprise. "You can't wait! He's going to the dam! He knows he's been discovered, and he's not going to wait. He's got explosives, and he's going to use them to blow up the dam. We have to stop him now!"

Alice looked at the two of them.

"I'll take it from here," she said in an authoritative voice. "You two get this man to the marina."

Mogi couldn't believe it. She wasn't going to do anything? She was going to just sit here and wait? He didn't understand. The man in the professor's houseboat was almost next to the dam. Once there, he'd blow it up! The whole thing! Millions would die!

Mogi couldn't stand it. Doing nothing right now was not an option.

He looked at Jennifer for a second. Then he planted his foot on the driver's seat, launched himself over the side, and stepped into the ranger's boat. In a flash, he whipped the connecting rope off the rail, reached over the seat, and shoved the throttle forward. This would have to be something else that they wouldn't tell Mom and Dad.

"Hey! HEY!" Alice yelled, reaching for the now

out-of-reach boat. She started fumbling for her pistol, but Jennifer jumped into the front seat and slammed the throttle forward. Alice went tumbling across the professor and onto the floor.

Oh, dear, Jennifer thought. What have we done?

CHAPTER 18

OW! This baby can move! Mogi was plastered back into the seat as the two huge outboard motors made the boat literally leap out of the water. He could see that the houseboat had reached the cliff next to the dam but could no longer see the man on top. Mogi curved out and brought the ranger boat in from an angle, trying to get a view of the front of the houseboat.

Suddenly, the windshield of the ranger boat exploded in a million pieces, showering Mogi with a splash of pain all over his arms and face. Glancing ahead as he ducked beneath the console, he saw the man on the deck aim a rifle at him. Another spray of bullets flew across the bow.

Mogi turned the wheel as hard as he could. A third spray of bullets hit the back of the boat, and one of the outboard motors jerked, smoke billowing from beneath the cover.

Cutting the boat back and forth to make for a

harder target, Mogi kept peeking over the dashboard to keep the houseboat in sight. Coming now from the opposite side, he saw the man leap into the speedboat tied to the back.

In a heartbeat, he started the motor and was racing across the lake.

The houseboat bobbed aimlessly in the water. It was clear that the man was racing away from the dam as fast as he could, which could mean only one thing —the explosives were ready to go off.

Mogi turned the ranger boat around, whipping through the plume of smoke pouring from the engine.

Just then, a sharp flash of light came from the front of the houseboat's pontoons, followed by a loud BOOM. A thick column of water shot into the air as the panel side of the houseboat began to tilt and the front dipped below the surface.

The pontoon on the other side rose out of the water, arced above the submerging side, and was held vertical in the water while the houseboat began to slowly sink beneath it. Wallowing in a crooked fashion as water spouted in a dozen different places, one side sank, leaving only the one pontoon floating above the water.

Mogi took some deep breaths. It was gone, just like that. All the professor's work. The books, the drawings, the photographs. And the sub. The man had succeeded in blowing up everything.

Wait a minute.

The explosives had to have been brought aboard the rental houseboat in the coolers. That's why there were so many, and why they were now all empty. There were many coolers, which meant there were a lot of explosives.

The explosion he had just witnessed was not all that big.

A chill ran down his back. The man had sunk the houseboat so that the rest of the explosives would be taken to the bottom of the lake, right at the base of the cliffs that supported the massive concrete dam.

Mogi kept the throttle up until he came close.

Something bobbed in the water. As he came closer, he recognized it.

The sub!

The guy must not have winched it up, Mogi thought.

As one pontoon sank and the other side of the boat arced into the air, the second pontoon had lifted itself up and over the sub, leaving it untouched, rocking back and forth in the water.

Mogi maneuvered the boat alongside the sub and then pulled the throttle back to idle.

Now what?

He looked ahead at the tall, massive concrete structure just a few hundred yards away. The explosives had been on the top of the houseboat, the professor had said, so they were now gone, dumped into the water as the houseboat had turned over.

Mogi turned and looked at the cliffs above him. They were not more than twenty yards away.

When the houseboat turned over, he reasoned, the explosives slid off the roof and sank straight down, surely having been connected to explode. If the cliff were like the others he saw while diving, there would be a slope beneath the water, a slope that was the cliff itself, which would end in a shelf just before the cliff continued to fall off toward the bottom. The explosives would have fallen right into the soft sediment of that shelf. If they exploded there, the impact might pound that slope to smithereens, causing the shelf to give way, which might cause the cliff to break off.

That shelf ran underwater all the way to the dam. If the shelf gave way, then the slope would give way, the cliff would break, and the dam would fracture. If it did, thousands of people would die, and the flooding would devastate millions more.

Thinking as quickly as he could, he saw only one way out: The explosives needed to be taken farther out into the lake. If they were away from the cliff, the explosion would be against the bottom of the lake, not against the cliff.

Mogi carefully straddled the railing of the ranger boat and gingerly stepped onto the sub's ballast tank. He opened the cockpit window and got into the submarine.

The explosives had to be on a timer. Maybe he had enough time to get them moved. He looked at his watch, lowered the cockpit glass, set the latches, flipped the power switches, and pushed the stick forward.

The sub gurgled as he watched the water flow over the glass above him.

CHAPTER 19

Alice was still fuming. All the action was happening over there and she was over here, stuck with people for whom she was now responsible. In a pathetic boat. Other rangers were racing to the scene, and she would miss all the action.

She pushed the motor to the max and headed for the marina. Without a radio, she couldn't even tell anyone what happened.

When the explosion went off in the distance, she fumed even more.

———

The first thing Mogi had to do was remember. He needed to remember everything the professor had said about the sub, plus everything he had seen when he was inside: what gauge measured what, what was balanced against something else, how the lights turned on, how the arms were used, how to move the sub down, up, sideways, backward, forward.

Fighting against the fear of not having time, he still closed his eyes and went back to three days before.

Remember.

His eyes opened not nearly as soon as he wished, but his memory had served him well. His memory was a gift, not a talent, his mom had told him.

Mogi looked at his watch, turned on the inside light, grabbed the throttle, and pushed it forward. The sub handled amazingly well. As misshapen as it appeared, he expected it to be clumsy and awkward underwater, but it glided smoothly. The reactions from the diver's motors on the back were quick and effective, and the control stick had just enough resistance to make controlling the sub easy to feel.

He let the sub sink. It got darker and colder, and there was no sound. He felt his way through the switches until he successfully turned on the outside lights, throwing a yellow glare on the dull, mud-covered cliff moving past him. The part of the cliff under the water was not as steep as he thought it would be, and he backed the sub away to not collide with it.

Through the glass of the canopy, he saw a dark blotch in the shimmering light above. It was the houseboat bobbing on the surface. He tried to stay directly beneath the blotch, hoping to follow the same path the explosives would have taken.

The water suddenly got murky, and Mogi jerked

back on the control stick just before he felt the sub hit the soft bottom. The sediment cloud that immediately surrounded him seemed like it would never settle down, and the outside lights only made things worse.

He backed the sub away and then circled around until he was in clear water again. He had probably hit a shelf, like he'd expected. The bottom had to be behind him, more toward the middle of the lake and much deeper.

But if he had hit the shelf below the cliff, then the explosives should have hit the same spot.

Where would they be?

It wasn't going to be easy. The lights of the sub were strong, but they shone only in front of the sub, forcing him to stay close to the shelf to keep any sense of direction. But when he was close to the mud-covered surface, the motors stirred up the sediment and the water became too clouded to see. Backing up and away a few times, Mogi finally found a level at which he could slowly move along the shelf and still see what was in front of him.

It seemed like an eternity, but it was only a minute later when he saw a jumbled mess of boxes, scrunched together and partially buried in the mud of the shelf.

Okay, he thought. This ought to be simple. I'll grab as many of the connecting wires between the boxes as I can, pick them up, and then back up. I'll take them toward the middle of the lake a full minute, which should be a couple of hundred yards, drop them, and get out of here.

The first part worked well. He pushed the manipulator arms against the boxes, tipping a couple over, and exposed enough wires to grab. He opened the fingers on the end of the arm, got them under the wires, and closed his grip.

Mogi pulled the arms up, pulled the stick back to go up, and pulled the throttle to go back. The submarine slid a couple of feet, jerked when the wires pulled tight, and then stopped completely when more of the boxes tightened against each other. He pulled the throttle back more, but the sub's only reaction was to tilt down as if it were anchored on its nose.

The boxes were too heavy for the sub to lift.

As cold as it was at this depth, Mogi started sweating.

Now what?

He glanced at his watch: Eighteen minutes had gone by since he had jumped into the sub.

How long was the timer set for?

Not allowing himself to think about it, he leveled the sub, pulled back on the throttle, and slowly rotated the control stick in one direction and then the other. The sub was wiggling, slowly creeping away from the slope.

Instead of picking the explosives up, he'd drag them across the shelf, drop them right at the edge, and then use the nose of the sub to push them into deeper water.

One minute, two minutes. The boxes felt like weights refusing to allow the sub to move, but as long as there was only a steady resistance, he figured it had to be working.

The sub began to gain momentum, moving him faster and farther from the muck stirred up by the boxes. Watching out the side of the sub, he saw that the water became clear and the ledge appeared beneath him.

Only at the last minute did he see the edge. He jammed the throttle forward.

Not soon enough.

The heavy boxes slipped over the rim of the ledge and fell into the darkness beneath him. The sub's nose was yanked downward, accelerating as the boxes continued to fall, their weight yanking him into the nothingness below.

As the sub's nose plummeted, Mogi fell out of the seat and into the front of the cockpit, crashing against the dashboard and window. His body slammed against the control stick, and the sub flailed against the much larger force of the explosives.

Mogi panicked, grabbing the air with his arms as his body pitched over the lights on the dashboard. Before he could think of anything to do, the boxes slammed into another shelf, the sub slammed into the boxes, and Mogi slammed even harder against the canopy.

Everything stopped.

Straining to hold his body in a constant position, Mogi moved the ballast controls so that the sub became level.

He got himself back into the pilot's seat, pushed his feet against the control panel, and shoved himself as far back into the seat cushion as he could. He was shivering uncontrollably, both from the cold and from the terror exploding inside him.

He screamed.

The sound was dull and hollow, confined by the close surfaces around him. His chest was heaving and he struggled to get a deep breath. He begged himself to settle down, to think, to focus, to get his mind right.

He had dropped way deeper, meaning that the explosives were closer to the thicker base of the original mesa.

If they went off now, the effect would be nothing compared to where they'd been.

Mission accomplished. Time to disconnect and go to the surface.

Mogi dropped the sub a couple of feet, pointed the nose toward the boxes, and moved closer. He opened the grips at the ends of the arms, turned the handles, and brought the arms closer to the cockpit.

But the wires from the boxes didn't slide off. He turned the arms to the side, rotated them, and tilted them down again.

The wires still didn't slide off.

He leaned forward, adjusted a light, and looked at the grips on the end of the arms. His heart sank. When the sub had slammed into the boxes, the wires had twisted into the fingers and bent the supports back. The whole front of the sub was a confusion of twisted arms and cables and wires.

The sub was caught.

Mogi pulled the throttle all the way back. The sub

jerked against the cables, fishtailing as the metal of the arms unfolded, twisted, and turned. He forced the water from the ballast tanks. That made the sub pivot straight up, which again threw Mogi out of his seat and against the dashboard. He listened to the motors thrash, trying to jerk the sub free. The muck around him clouded the water, and he looked out into swirling clouds of liquid dirt.

The sub strained for the surface, but the mechanical arms did not break, did not let go, and the wiring entangled in the fingers did not pull apart.

It lifted and dragged one, then two of the boxes, but did not release them.

Mogi did not know what to do.

The lights began to flicker, and the whir of the motors decreased. The batteries were almost exhausted from having worked so hard. In a few seconds, he'd be in the dark, in the cold, without hope. He was no longer in a submarine, he was in a coffin.

Mogi shivered violently, struggling to breathe. He screamed and began to sob.

What had he done?

CHAPTER 20

A lice found a solution. When the explosion went off, several of the early morning fishing boats had turned and sped in its direction.

Using her hat and whistle, she flagged one down and asked the pilot to take Jennifer and the injured man back to the medical office in the marina. With the amount of blood splashed all over the victim, it wasn't hard to convince them that it was urgent.

Having moved the stricken man over the rails and into the other boat, Alice sat back in the driver's seat and prepared to go after her ranger boat.

That's when Jennifer jumped into the McDowells' passenger seat.

"You cannot come with me!" Alice yelled. "This is official business!"

"I'm not leaving my brother!" Jennifer yelled back.

"And this is my boat, so it is also *my* business!"

Alice had already lost enough time, and she'd lose more if she argued any further.

"Well, then, hang on!" she shouted and shoved the throttle forward.

───────

It was quiet and dark. Mogi was lonelier than he had ever felt in his life.

In the last of the cockpit light, Mogi put enough water back into the ballast tanks to make the sub sit level in the surrounding darkness. He worked on the cockpit window, undoing the latches and pushing on the glass. If he could get out, he could swim to the surface. There was a dive tank and respirator behind the seat that the professor kept for emergencies. He could try it, though he was pretty sure he could hold his breath long enough. At least he had taken off his weight belt as he and Jennifer had shifted the professor to their speedboat.

That seemed so long ago.

But the window wouldn't budge no matter what he did—the outside pressure wouldn't let the canopy shift a millimeter.

He tried to break the glass, hoping that the inside of the sub would flood and he'd have enough time for the window to be worked free. But the glass didn't even scratch.

He sat back in the seat and shivered.

It was a fighter jet, stupid. These windows are

made for flying a zillion miles an hour. They're probably even bulletproof.

Mogi remembered the movie *Apollo 13*. What was Tom Hanks's character saying during an interview? He'd been over the Sea of Japan, in a fighter jet, at night, and he was returning to land on an aircraft carrier. But he was lost. It was a completely dark night, he couldn't see the carrier, his instruments had stopped working, and he was low on fuel.

Then his lights went out.

So he was up in the air, flying blind, in the dark, running out of gas.

But he looked below him and saw that the sea had a ribbon of bright green across it. It was the glow of the algae that had been churned up in the propellers of the huge carrier.

All the pilot had to do was follow the path of the glowing algae. It would lead him to the carrier. It would take him home.

Tom Hanks's character was talking about waiting, and being aware, and keeping an attitude that would allow him to take advantage of the unexpected. If the lights inside his cockpit hadn't gone out, it would never have been dark enough for him to see the algae. He would have had to eject. Way out in the middle of the dark, cold ocean.

Eject!

Mogi caught his breath. What had the professor said about the cockpit seat? That he had left it just as it had been restored? If the original owners hadn't bothered to remove the parachute when they salvaged the jet...could the ejector still be working? The professor said that he had done nothing beyond removing the parachute. If the ejector mechanism still worked, it would blow the canopy off the cockpit and shoot the pilot's seat straight up.

Mogi felt around between his legs, running his fingers around the bottom of the seat. He felt a handle and lifted it up between his legs so that both of his hands fit around it.

He felt around and hooked the seat belts, pressed his arms close to his body, closed his eyes, prayed, and pulled the handle.

———

Alice had run the boat for all it was worth, but she was still the last one on the scene.

Two other monster ranger boats hovered around the area of the partially sunken houseboat. Alice's boat, one engine still belching smoke, had drifted away, bumping against the shore. A ranger was on board, wielding a fire extinguisher.

The houseboat itself was mostly submerged, with only part of a single pontoon still sticking out of the water, bobbing like a fishing lure. A ranger had lassoed the end of the pontoon and was running a rope to an inflated WARNING bag. If the houseboat sank fully, that bag would remain on top to indicate the wreck below.

Alice maneuvered next to a ranger boat, jumped

across to it, and then told Jennifer to move out of the area and return to the marina.

"But what about my brother?" she cried.

"When you find him, he needs to move out of the area too."

Disgusted, Jennifer hit the throttle and sped away. For about fifty yards. Then she throttled the engine back to idle, stood up in the seat, and scanned the water all around the wreck. She had watched Mogi climb into the sub's cockpit but had no idea what he planned to do.

"Come on, Mogi!" she cried, finally letting her tears flow. "Come on!"

A hundred yards behind her, toward the center of lake, a fountain of water suddenly squirted into the air.

Shooting through the top of the spout was a large, dark object that looked like a chair, and out of the chair, launched as if from a cannon, a body was slung into the air, the seat belts automatically releasing at the last moment. Making a not-so-graceful arc, the body fell back into the water.

It seemed like only a body. As limp as a rag doll.

Jennifer hit the throttle and turned the boat toward the spout.

In a split second, the boat lifted into the air.

A huge bubble of water, two hundred yards wide, lifted not only Jennifer and her boat out of the water, but every floating object nearby. Even the overturned houseboat lurched in the water, rolled over, and rolled back again.

A huge, dull noise, like a massive *whump*, erupted from the bubble and echoed throughout the Lake Powell basin.

The Outlaw had finally succeeded.

Jennifer was thrown into the back of the boat as it bucked through the massive waves caused by the explosion. With the throttle still in the maximum-speed position, it jostled and jerked and skipped as the outboard's propeller plunged in and out of the foam. She fought to get herself back into the seat, slogging through the knee-deep muddy water that now sloshed in the boat. She pulled the throttle back and desperately scanned the water around the spot where she had seen the spout.

She saw a flash of red—Mogi had pulled the cord on his emergency inflation vest.

Jennifer dove over the side and into the water.

CHAPTER 21

Mogi felt terrible, but he wasn't quite sure why. He slowly opened his eyes. The light was good, but it felt like someone was sitting on his head.

"Hey," Jennifer said.

It wasn't a hospital—there wasn't enough equipment—but something like it. Maybe a clinic? And what did she say?

He put his hands up to his face but only felt bandages.

His hands, his arms, his face.

That's not good, he thought.

"You need to be careful with those. They used up their supply, so we don't have anymore. That exploding windshield really did a number on your skin."

What did she say?

"What?"

Jennifer moved her face directly in front of him.

"And in addition to being cut to pieces and almost drowning, you lost both your eardrums."

"What?"

He was beginning to get the idea. He could see her lips move but heard only a muffled noise. It was like being under a pillow.

"What?"

"Eardrums repair themselves quickly, so his hearing will return soon," the nurse said to Jennifer and Mr. and Mrs. Franklin. "However, it's going to take some time for him to get his balance back. A lot of water got into his inner ears, and it will take a while for them to drain."

CHAPTER 22

THREE WEEKS AFTER THE BOMBING

I f Hawthorne's houseboat had looked like a garage sale prize before, it was definitely now king of the junkyard. After being pulled from the lake, it was hauled to an empty lot past Wahweap Marina and dumped next to a large building that housed a boat repair shop. Yellow police tape surrounded it, wrapped on temporary posts.

"Only one pontoon blew up?" Mogi asked. "Why didn't he blow up both?"

"He meant to," the professor answered. "The FBI found a charge attached to the second pontoon, and they're guessing that the two had been connected. Either the guy messed up or a wire came loose or something, but only one charge went off. If both pontoons had been destroyed, the entire boat would have sunk, taking the sub with it."

The professor, Mogi, and Jennifer walked around

the houseboat, mesmerized by seeing the damage up close. It had been set upright, but it was tipped and twisted in both directions because the ripped pontoon was bent in, around, and under the cabin. The front corner of the cabin was missing, a large ragged hole now showing the front bedroom and bathroom. The solar panels close by had been broken off and hung by a few twisted bolts.

The FBI had taken over the houseboat, wanting to get fingerprints and to capture any evidence that had been left behind. Since the houseboat had hung upside down in a lake for three days before they pulled it out, they didn't find anything.

Once the FBI and Homeland Security had wrapped up the paperwork, the houseboat and its contents had been officially returned to the professor. Finding it a good time for a reunion, he had invited Mogi and Jennifer to return to the lake. After spending so many summers preoccupied with his Butch Cassidy search, he had found his contact with the two teens refreshing.

They climbed up onto the awkwardly slanted deck.

Mogi used his shoulder to shove the cabin's back door open, and the three carefully stepped inside.

"I'm so sorry, Professor," Jennifer said. "All your work, your pictures, your books, your research…"

"And I am so, so sorry about your submarine," Mogi said for the umpteenth time.

Hawthorne laughed. "Have no sorrow, my friends. Imagine how I would feel if the man had succeeded with his grand scheme. Besides, I can always build another one.

"Although"—he laughed again—"the official warnings I got for having an unregistered boat on Lake Powell makes me believe that I'm out of the submarine business. They'll be watching me."

"What about your research? What about proving your theory about Butch Cassidy?" Jennifer asked.

The professor picked up a pile of papers from the floor, but they dissolved into a foul-smelling slop.

"The research is still good," he said, "and I had copies of 90 percent of everything. I can replace all the books. The only real loss is the pictures from this summer, and especially that last morning. I might have had a breakthrough, but my project is over, regardless."

Jennifer and Mogi stepped through the mess into the bedroom area. Mud covered everything, paper was hardly distinguishable, and the computer lay under the mud-soaked mattress.

"Well," the professor said, "I'll take the computer. Maybe somebody can get something off the hard drive. Everything else, I declare unrecoverable and forever lost."

Mogi helped set the computer outside on the deck.

The three friends walked back through the cabin, found themselves semi-comfortable sitting spots on the back deck, and sat, hanging their legs over the side.

"What did you mean about a breakthrough?" Jennifer asked. "Did you find something?"

Mogi leaned close to them. His hearing had mostly returned, but sounds were still muffled. It took watching their lips at the same time to understand all the words. His bandages were off, but he had to spread an ointment on his skin every night. When he coughed, he still tasted mud.

The professor tucked his hands under his thighs and leaned forward. "On the morning I was kidnapped, I took the sub down to the rock faces on the cliffs at the entrance to the canyon. Something your brother said the day before was bothering me. He asked about how thick the sediment was at the bottom of the lake. I had always guessed that the mud was four or five feet deep and assumed that any mark left by Butch would have been higher up the wall than that.

"If the mark were covered by mud, there wouldn't be much I could do about it. But, just to see what would happen, I went over to the most obvious entrance to the canyon. I turned the sub around, backed into the area, and then shoved the throttle all the way forward. The thrust from the motors blew some of the silt away from the rock. That was encouraging, so I did it several times. I opened up an area about twenty feet long and probably two or three feet below where I had previously taken pictures.

"And, by golly, there were some handprints I hadn't seen before."

"Handprints?"

"A very common image in the Southwest. The handprint is sometimes viewed as the most personal mark left by early people. You put your hand up against the rock and either chipped out around the hand, or scraped the outline, or used charcoal or paint, or put some dark-colored liquid in your mouth and spewed over the hand to leave the outline of the hand.

"But one of these handprints was different. All the handprints I've seen, including those in books and photographs, have the fingers spread out, like this." He held his hand upright, with his fingers separated. "What I found on the rock was a right handprint with the fingers closed, like this." He held up his right hand with the fingers and thumb closed together, as if ready to give a salute. "And it was big, maybe twice the size of the other handprints. I looked at it a long time before I photographed it."

Mogi immediately reached for his phone, but Jennifer's hand fell over his.

"Hey, I forgot—" he began, but was immediately interrupted.

"That sounds important," Jennifer said as her hand kept Mogi from pulling out his phone. "Do you think it means something?"

"But remember our—" Mogi interjected.

"Something important?" Jennifer continued, looking at her brother with a look that told him to shut up.

"Oh, I expect not," the professor responded. "I'm probably not remembering other instances where pictographs or petroglyphs had the same style of handprint. But the important thing is that I hadn't really considered that there would be markings buried beneath the mud.

"That's where my project finally, truly, ended." He laughed. "Do you know how much work it would be to go back to all the places I've taken pictures of, move two or three feet of sediment out of the way, and do it all over again?

"I don't think so. I had a moment of truth and decided that it was time to wrap it up and spend my summers doing something else. Finding that mysterious mark left by Butch Cassidy, when it might not exist at all, is a nice idea, but it's time to let William T. Phillips keep his secrets."

CHAPTER 23

SOMEWHERE IN EASTERN
WASHINGTON, 1932

"You shouldn't lead him on like that. He's just a little boy."

"Oh, posh, Etta. I'm just having fun. Besides, little boys grow up to be men, and men ought to know about such things."

"Boys grow up to be men, and they grow up to be the men who raised them. Talking about the old days and telling him all about banks and trains and how noble the outlaw was when he fought against the lawyers and the railroad owners isn't just telling him stories. It's telling him how to live."

"Darn right it's how he ought to live! Besides, he's not going to remember half of what I tell him, and he'll figure out soon enough not to believe the other half. Maybe banks and bankers have changed, and we don't have those rotten scoundrels in the railroads anymore, but there will always be other scoundrels. A young boy needs to know where the line is, how to stand up for hisself, and how to be a good person in spite of what people expect him to act like.

"And, besides, we did all right, didn't we? We're good people, aren't we? We did a lot of good for people. It was only a few that wanted to hang us."

The woman moved from the breadboard where she had been kneading dough and draped her arms around the man.

"Now, now," the man complained, "don't be getting that white stuff all over my duds. I have a certain image to maintain, you know, a distinguished, older gentleman such as myself."

"I wouldn't waste the flour," she said as she crossed her forearms in front of him, carefully holding her flour-laden hands away. "But listening to you is sometimes trying to my ears. You have so many words, it fills them up."

The man grinned, turned his head, and kissed her on the cheek.

"All those words, well, that's my way. I was always the brains and the words. It wasn't luck, you know, it was, well, talent. My talent lies in the area of brain power, I do believe, and I know how to express myself so that I am clearly understood. Ain't that right?"

The woman laughed. "Oh, it's very true. You always had the brains and the words, but usually not enough of one and too much of the other."

They both laughed. She moved back to the breadboard.

"Are you going to let Bill tell everything?" she asked.

"Ah, you'd like him better if you'd give him a chance," the man replied. "He's all right. He just, well, words don't come natural to him like they do to me, so I help him a bit. And I've told him a lot, that's for sure. He and I, you know, were in prison in Wyoming together. That's where I met him. He'd listen to me for hours, hanging on my every word. I'd hate to stop now."

"He's not going to let on the truth about who's writing what?"

"Hah! Nobody'd believe him! The man wants to put down my stories, all together in one place, which I think would look good myself. Somebody ought to write about everything we did. We were famous, from here to the tip of South America."

"Oh, I know that you and Harry were famous," she replied. "I got to hang around while the two of you did all the work. But I would rather Bill kept his mouth shut. I'm not up to running anymore, and I'm not about to let you do it either. I'm not going to watch you get arrested and then try to talk some judge into why you shouldn't be punished for it, your action having been the noble thing to do."

The man grinned. "Now, with respect to that," he said, "I am absolutely, one hundred percent in agreement with you. I have no desire to be anything other than an obscure country gentleman who people think hasn't done a darn thing exciting in his whole life. I think Bill should say he's the famous Butch Cassidy if he wants to. Then people could chase him, if they was still of a mind to do so."

"He doesn't look a thing like you. Nobody would believe him."

"Yeah, well, even I don't look a thing like I used to, and he's not that bad-looking a guy. 'Course, he's not as good-looking as me, but who is? If he wants to let on that he's me, I say go ahead. Let him be bothered with all those people wanting to sally up to a famous person, and let him watch over his shoulder for those Pinkertons, who I am sure are still sore about me giving them the slip. I'm done with that life."

The screen door whipped open and banged against the house. A boy of about nine rushed in and went to the man seated at the table.

"I did it! I roped 'im good!"

"Well, now, that's something to be proud of," the man said as he patted the boy on the back. "How many tries?"

"One."

"One?"

"Two. I tried twice before I did it."

"Twice before you did it means you threw the rope three times. You needed three times?"

"Well, yes, sir. It was at least three times."

"You mean three times is what you tried, or you mean it was more than three times?"

"I, uh, once I got the rope right and the goat stopped moving, I got 'im good."

"Oh, ho! Now it's three times after the goat stopped moving, which means you were trying to rope him before he had stopped moving. Now, how many times while the goat was moving, and we'll add that to the three times after he stopped moving. How many times?"

"Uh, uh—"

"Okay, come here," the man said. "Stand up tall and look at me."

The man positioned the boy in front of him.

"Up now, stand up straight, like you're proud. Be tall. Now raise your right hand. No, don't let your fingers get all splayed out like that. Hold them straight up and keep them all together."

The man raised the boy's arm until it was up and away from his body and then fashioned the hand with the fingers and thumb together.

"Now we need a Bible. You have a Bible? No Bible. I tell you what." The man reached over and took a biscuit freshly cut from the dough. "We'll pretend this is a Bible, okay? Here you go. You take your left hand. No, no, leave the right one up where we had it. Keep your fingers and thumb together. Now, your left hand goes on top of the Bible, which looks a lot like a biscuit, but we know it's a Bible."

The boy stood before the man, right hand raised, with his left hand on the biscuit.

"This is what we call taking the sacred oath. You see it in a court of law all the time. The judge wants you to tell the truth, so he makes you hold your hands just like this, to swear to everybody in the courtroom, and to God, and to the judge in particular, that you're about to tell the truth and nothing but the truth. You got it?"

The boy nodded.

"Okay. Well, then, I think we're ready. I'll be the judge, and you be the poor guy on the hook for answering questions. Here we go. How many times, sir, did you have to throw the rope before you successfully and completely roped the goat so that the goat was completely and entirely roped?"

The boy giggled.

"Uh, I...uh, well, it was a bunch of times, your honor."

"That's what I thought. You are hereby judged completely guilty of being innocent and unpracticed in the art of roping goats. You are hereby sentenced to practicing with said goat or other goats, as time allows. Case closed. You may step from the bench and now proceed to rope the goat again to see if you can, hereby, rope the goat with fewer attempts than you previously attempted."

The man turned the laughing boy toward the door.

"Taking a sacred oath?" the woman said with a skeptical tone.

"Absolutely! I know it well, having had to use it several times. Too many times in my eyes and probably not enough in the eyes of my enemies."

Etta placed the cutout biscuits on a sheet and slid them into the oven, including the one that was now more holy, it having been, for a short time, a Bible.

"Time?"

The man reached into the pocket of his vest and pulled out a pocket watch. It was an old Elgin, a fancy one with a circle of diamonds around the face, and it had what at the time was state-of-the-art for pocket watches—a winding stem.

He looked carefully at it, gave the woman the time, and then closed it and returned it to his pocket. He patted it gently.

You always want to take care of your watch, the man thought. A watch represents a lot of memories.

CHAPTER 24

PRESENT DAY

"Why didn't you let me show him the picture of the hand?"

Jennifer slowed the car as she hit the unpaved portion of Highway 261, right at the top of the Moki Dugway. Thirty or so miles more and they'd be home.

"Did you hear the tone of his voice when he was telling about being done with looking for Butch's mark?" she asked her brother.

"Uh, well, not particularly. I could barely hear words, much less tone of voice."

"You'll have to take my word for it, then. When he was talking about not building another submarine, about not repeating his search by moving mud from the walls, and about letting the whole idea go, I heard relief in his voice. Like somebody who had finally been freed from something."

"But we could have shown him the picture. It sounds exactly like what we saw. If so, it could be his answer."

"That might be true. But for him to publish something that claimed that the hand was the mark, people would be all over him to search the east entrances to all the canyons to show that the mark was unique. And somebody else would want the image photographed, so he'd have to find some way to go back down underwater and find it again. Then somebody would disagree, and then and then and then...

"His voice told me that he was happy to be done with it. Showing him the picture we took of the big hand would have committed him to more of the same work for the rest of his life. And, even if it turned out to be believable, all he would have proven is that Butch Cassidy didn't die as history says. But he still could not prove how he actually died."

Mogi had been leaning toward her, watching her lips.

"Well, okay. You're probably right. I guess now he can do other things.

"But more importantly, did the FBI tell him what's going to happen to the comic books? I wouldn't mind getting my hands on some of them. Or all of them, for that matter. It was quite a collection."

"Nope," Jennifer replied. "They'll probably sit around in a cardboard box for a while and then slowly disappear due to all the FBI men who can't keep their hands off them. I swear, I do not understand comic books."

"It's a man thing," Mogi said. "Deep inside, every man wants to be a superhero and see himself in a picture with words like *BAPP*, *SOCKO*, and *KAPOW* in little spikey balloons around him."

The man who called himself Dr. Death, Outlaw, would never see himself in a comic book. He'd had a plan, but it fizzled in the end, and so did he. His abandoned speedboat was discovered puttering in a circle past Antelope Point, up a canyon a few miles east of the dam, nearly out of gas. The FBI conjectured that the man simply jumped out while it was still going. They figured that he sank all his guns and equipment, walked out at some marina, and then hitchhiked his way back to wherever he had come from.

The FBI immediately put him on the Most Wanted List, which would have pleased him, but his name came off the next day when he was arrested.

Dr. Death had indeed come out of the river at the campground at Antelope Point. He'd explained to a soft-hearted soul that his boat was out of gas and had gotten a ride into town. However, anticipating that he would soon run out of money, he had brought his dive equipment with him, expecting that it would be worth a lot of money at a pawn shop. But before he even made it through the door, word had spread through all official police channels, and the pawn shop, assisted by the State Police, made Dr. Death a deal he could not refuse. A deal that would probably have him back counting eight steps up and eight steps back for a long, long time.

The FBI refused his request to return his comic books.

———

After that, it was all over. National devastation had not occurred, so the explosion at the lake was minor news.

How close it had truly come to disaster stayed within the circle of those involved. Everyone went back to normal life, and the incident went to the back page of everybody's memory.

Except for Alice. She was still fuming over her boat being taken away, and she tried to convince her bosses to bring charges against the Franklins for interfering with an investigation. She was put back to reading the mail.

The dam suffered no damage. It didn't even shudder.

The powerful shock waves of the explosion pounded the bottom cliffs around the lake, but there was enough sediment covering everything that it was like hitting a pillow.

The shock waves moving through the water spread out and did no damage beyond killing hundreds of fish.

Having returned to the lake to visit with the professor, the Franklins were happy to be going home.

Mogi found a couple of the business cards he had pocketed from the search of the houseboat in White Canyon Bay. He offered one to Jennifer, but she wanted no souvenirs connected to Dr. Death, Outlaw. That left him silent as they headed down the Dugway incline and approached their town of Bluff, Utah.

From the top of Cedar Mesa, the roadway dropped more than eight hundred feet to the floor of the valley below. In the distance, several spires of sandstone stood majestically over the mostly flat land, giving the landscape an other-worldly feel.

Winding down the steep road carved out of the side of the sandstone mesa, Mogi found himself happy, for once, that his hometown was as dry as a bone.

A LOOK AT: THE LADY IN WHITE
(A MOGI FRANKLIN MYSTERY 7)

Uncover Haunted Secrets and Face the Past in *The Lady in White*—A Spine-Tingling Middle-Grade Mystery Adventure!

Mogi Franklin's summer job as a cowboy on one of the largest ranches in New Mexico was supposed to be simple —ride horses, work cattle, and enjoy the wide-open spaces —but when hundreds of cattle start dying under mysterious circumstances, Mogi's search for answers leads him to an eerie, abandoned mansion along the Canadian River—and the ghostly figure of a lady in white who haunts its halls.

As Mogi digs deeper, he uncovers the story of a boy kidnapped by Comanche warriors in 1871 and a mother's desperate, undying love. But the past isn't the only thing haunting the ranch. Mogi soon finds himself caught in a dangerous plot that threatens the land and lives of everyone around him. To save the ranch, he must confront not just the enemies of the present, but the lingering shadows of the past.

Can Mogi unravel the secrets of the past before it's too late?

AVAILABLE APRIL 2025

ABOUT THE AUTHOR

New Mexico-based **Donald Willerton** is the author of *Death in the Tallgrass*, the winner of the Western Writers of America 2024 SPUR Award for Western Historical Fiction, a finalist in the 2024 American Fiction Awards, and a finalist in the 2024 Storytrade Book Awards. He has written a ten-book Middle Grade/Young Adult mystery series located in the Southwest, two contemporary thrillers, and a fictional World War II adventure novel.

To finance his writing, he used his degrees in physics and computer science as a scientist, manager, and computer specialist, but has always let his curiosity, imagination, and passion for history keep his head aligned with his heart.

www.ingramcontent.com/pod-product-compliance
Lightning Source LLC
Chambersburg PA
CBHW011434170626
46808CB00010B/3164